SHADOW OF THE LOCKED

RESURRECTING MAGIC - BOOK THREE

KEARY TAYLOR

Copyright © 2020 Keary Taylor

All rights reserved. Except as permitted under the U.S. Copyright act of 1976, no part of this publication may be reproduced, distributed, or transmitted in any form or by any means, or stored in a database or retrieval system, without the prior written permission of the author.

First Edition: August 2020

Cover art by Orina Kafe

The characters and events portrayed in this book are fictitious. Any similarity to real persons, living or dead, is coincidental and not intended by the author.

Taylor, Keary, 1987-
Shadow of the Locked (Resurrecting Magic): a novel / by Keary Taylor.
— 1st ed.

ALSO BY KEARY TAYLOR

THE RESURRECTING MAGIC SERIES
Rise of the Mage

Keeper of the Lost

THE BLOOD DESCENDANTS UNIVERSE
House of Royals Saga

Garden of Thorns Trilogy

Crown of Death Saga

THE FALL OF ANGELS TRILOGY

THE NERON RISING SAGA

THE EDEN TRILOGY

THE McCAIN SAGA

WHAT I DIDN'T SAY

Also by T.L. Keary (thriller/suspense pen name)

THREE HEART ECHO

OUR LAST CONFESSION

SKIN AND BONE

CHAPTER ONE

"Keep it down," Nathaniel said as he quickly looked out the window at the dark sky. "It's the middle of the night."

How could he ask us to stay quiet? To stay calm? A man had just magically emerged from a book.

"You say…" Olin said, and I could tell his thoughts were spinning out as he tried to get a grasp on everything happening. "You say magic has been gone for centuries?"

Nathaniel nodded, coming to sit on the chair just in front of the man out of time. "Yes. Though, we're having a hard time piecing the history together. We would like to ask you some questions."

I looked over at Borden. There was still electricity sparking between his hands, and with the dead serious way he was staring at Olin, I knew he was ready to do anything if the man moved or breathed wrong. I was really grateful for that.

Then again, there were six of us, and only one of him.

"I don't…" Olin said, his voice trailing off. "It doesn't make any sense." Because he was watching Borden with caution as well, Olin slowly climbed to his feet. He looked around the hotel room, bewildered and confused. He gripped the doorknob, and walked out into the night, immediately followed by Borden and Nathaniel.

"A man just popped out of a book," Poppy said, leaning over toward me. Her eyes were wide and terrified. "Judging from the reaction of everyone in the room, this isn't something that's happened before?"

"Definitely not," I said, shaking my head.

"Definitely don't want it to happen again," Mary-Beth said, looking through the door at Olin, who looked around, taking in the small city we were in the middle of.

"Is this what your daily lives are like?" Poppy asked. "Constant surprises and wild magical discoveries?"

A laugh actually bubbled from my chest. "Yes and no. Because we still have so much to learn, there are certainly frequent discoveries. But people springing from sealed books found in your mother's secret stash of books? No. That isn't really the norm."

Poppy shook her head. "And I thought being a flight attendant was an exciting lifestyle. Next you're going to tell me you know how to make people levitate and trick them into believing they're the Queen of England."

Mary-Beth and I looked at each other, and a little laugh escaped my lips.

"You could totally do those things, couldn't you?" Poppy asked with a disbelieving shake of her head.

"Basically, yes," I said.

Just then I heard gravel stirring outside and Olin walked back in, followed by Nathaniel and Borden.

"It's a lot to take in," Nathaniel said. "Don't let it overwhelm you." He closed the door behind them. Nathaniel indicated the chair for Olin. "Why don't we go through what you know first. It was the present for you. Can you please tell me about our past?"

I studied Olin as he looked around at all of us once more. He bore a fairly long beard, and hair that was longer as well. Because of it, it was difficult to tell how old he really was. Maybe mid-forties? He had broad shoulders and weathered hands that spoke of hard work. And there was an intensity in his eyes. It was the kind that was hard to read.

"You truly do not know of the Lock of Sandris?" he asked, looking around at everyone.

"Please, start there," Mary-Beth asked, sounding desperate.

Olin held her eyes for several long moments, hesitating before he gave information to people he didn't know, people he had no idea if he could trust or not.

"Euan Sandris was born to two magical parents forty or so years ago," Olin began, and the second he started telling the story, I felt gooseflesh crawling up over my scalp. "They were a powerful family. But they were not good people. They exercised their abilities to take advantage of the village around them. They murdered. They took souls. They did what they saw fit."

This was not the kind of story I wanted to hear when learning the history of my kind.

"But not all children turn out like their parents," Olin continued. "Euan was powerful, every bit like his parents, only more so. Watching them as he grew up, he hated them, and everything they did. He began to see magic as a curse. As evil. As something that should not exist in this world."

Olin looked out the window, even though it was too dark to see anything outside. He shook his head. "I know not how he did it. But over years, he practiced his own kind of magic. He learned how to lock it."

"What does that mean?" Mary-Beth asked.

Olin met her eyes, and I could actually pinpoint the moment when he understood why she was asking. "It means that he could block a witch from their magic. He could not erase their blood, but he could make it so they could not use it. Almost as if they were any other human on the planet."

"Euan Sandris was stripping mages of their magic?" Nathaniel asked.

Olin nodded. "And his parents were his first test subjects."

The weight in the room grew twice as heavy and suddenly, my mouth was dry.

"His infamy grew as he traveled throughout Scotland," Olin continued. "And even more so as he visited England. He gained followers, other witches, mages, who believed as he did. He taught them. And they took magic, locking it away."

My eyes slid over to Mary-Beth, who watched Olin with rapt attention.

"He was feared for eight long years," Olin said, and his tone grew dark. "There were stories and songs about him. Because once your magic was locked, no one knew how to unlock it. He was the devil himself to us. And then it happened."

From the distant look in his eyes, I knew whatever he said next would send chills down my spine.

"He poisoned the entire world," Olin continued. "In one powerful spell, he locked half of all magic wielders, in one fell swoop."

"Half?" Nathaniel asked. I could practically see the gears spinning in his head, furious and hungry for more knowledge.

Olin met his eyes and nodded. "Half. There were already few of us. All of us had lived through some kind of witch hunt because we weren't powerful enough, seen our friends and family members burned at the stake when they weren't watching their backs. There weren't many of us. And then he locked away half of all magic."

I looked over at Mary-Beth again.

Magic was inherited. It came through the blood.

She had magic. We knew she did.

But hers was locked away.

"Why only half?" Borden asked.

Olin looked up at him. "Do not misunderstand. If he'd been able to, Euan Sandris would have locked magic for everyone in the entire world."

"Why didn't he?" my father asked.

"Because he obliterated himself in the process of trying," Olin answered bleakly.

The room was silent for several long moments.

I tried not to picture it, but it was all I could see. A dark ritual done, powerful magic surging. Ill intent to steal all magic and take it away from the earth. And then it all going wrong, and him being obliterated into nothing.

"The reality of what he had done was immediate," Olin said. "My wife could no longer do what she once could. My father had been locked. Half of my aunts and uncles, cousins. For the past fifteen years, we have been trying to find a way to unlock magic."

The question hung in the air but remained unspoken. Had they?

"In these fifteen years, no one has found a solution." Olin's words condemned Mary-Beth.

Everyone was silent for a long few moments after that. We had just learned so much new information.

There was so much weight to it. There were wars and lives lost and bloodshed. Witch hunts and spells and lives ruined.

And now? Now there were just the five of us.

"So, I guess it's just my bad luck?" Mary-Beth asked, breaking the silence. "There are five of you who aren't locked. And me. Just me who drew the short stick."

She rose to her feet and walked out of the room.

"Mary-Beth," I said, my tone exasperated. I took a step toward her, but I knew, she needed her space to grieve.

"At least she hasn't been able to do magic from the start," Olin pointed out. "You can't imagine the grief my loved ones went through in losing it. For my wife…" He trailed off and I could see the grief settling into him. "For her, it was too much. Losing her magic was like losing her life. She felt she lost her worth. In the end, she took her own life."

The words were actually shocking. They hit my heart like one of Borden's electrical currents.

"I'm so sorry," Nathaniel offered sympathetically.

I could picture it, to some degree. If all this were to be taken away? How would that affect me? What would that do to my self-worth?

She might not have ever been able to do it, but still, my heart went out to Mary-Beth.

Olin looked over at Nathaniel. "You say magic has been lost. How did it happen?"

And so, Nathaniel did what he did best. He taught Olin what had happened, as far as we could tell. How there was a surge of witch hunts. How we lost any proof of witches after that. How magic went quiet, to the point of being forgotten.

Then, more than two hundred years later, he discovered a book. He found the rest of us who could do what he could.

By the time Nathaniel was finished telling Olin everything we knew, it was four AM. I was leaned up against a headboard, barely awake. Mary-Beth eventually returned and now was softly snoring next to me. And everyone else looked utterly exhausted.

"I think this is enough for one night," Dad said, and I was exceptionally grateful for it. "We can talk more later. But we have another shuttle to catch tomorrow after lunch. Everyone needs to get some sleep."

"You can sleep in our room," Nathaniel said to Olin.

From the look Borden was giving Olin, I wasn't sure he approved of Nathaniel's invitation. But he didn't say anything.

"Goodnight," Dad said as he bent down and pressed a kiss to my forehead.

"Night," I said, watching as all the men walked out of our room.

"Thanks again for letting me stay with you tonight," Poppy said.

I chuckled as I rolled over to look at her lying on the

other bed. "You're pretty much a superhero of calm in my book. All of this and you're still sticking around?"

She shrugged and smiled. "I have a feeling with all of you, life will never be boring again. Sounds like a pretty good way to spend my time to me."

I shook my head and smiled, amazed once more at her.

"Goodnight, Margot," Poppy said through a massive yawn.

"Night," I whispered through the dark.

And even though I knew I wasn't going to sleep well, I closed my eyes, and told myself to let it all go for tomorrow.

CHAPTER TWO

I didn't wake up until well after eleven. And then I only woke because I could hear Mary-Beth and Poppy talking, trying to be quiet.

Feeling like an absolute zombie, I dragged myself out of the bed and got in the shower. I got dressed. Did my hair. Brushed my teeth.

And at noon, there was a knock on the door.

Mary-Beth opened it to find my dad there.

"We're grabbing lunch and then it's back on the bus," he said. I didn't miss the way his eyes cast throughout the room, looking for any signs of danger or harm, even though he had no reason to think there would be. He was a father, first and always. And now it was like he had a whole slew of other kids to take care of.

"Be out in a few minutes," I said from the counter where I gathered up my things.

He nodded and walked away.

I was actually really grateful for the chaos and the crowded room as Poppy, Mary-Beth and I got ready to leave. I'd been an only child and all growing up, I had wished for a sister to play with. It was a passing thought, one I'd never let consume me, but it had always been there, in the background, wistful and contemplative.

Here, in this room, I had found two sisters.

"Ready?" Poppy asked as she stood in the doorway, her things all packed into her bag.

"I am starving," Mary-Beth said as she breezed through the door, one mission in mind.

"Thanks," I offered with a smile as I walked through the door. And together, the three of us headed to the diner across the street.

For the first time, it hit me. As I looked around and took in the cobblestone road and the lush green hills that rolled around me, I really realized I was in Scotland. This girl who had never left the East Coast, never traveled more than a few hundred miles from home, was in another country, all the way across the Atlantic Ocean.

A smile pulled on my lips as we walked up to the doors and slipped inside.

The boys were already at a table toward the back of the diner. We parked our bags out of the way, and I sank down into the seat next to Nathaniel, my heart instantly climbing into my throat. A pang of longing shot through me when my thigh brushed against his as I settled into my seat.

It took everything I had in me not to reach for his hand beneath the table, or to lean into him and press my lips to his.

But I just wished everyone a good morning.

"Looks like someone has gone on a shopping trip this morning," Mary-Beth said with a raised eyebrow cast in Olin's direction.

"Arthur and Nathaniel were very gracious in letting me borrow a few items," Olin said, looking down at himself dressed in modern clothes. "I will confess, the clothes of this century are far more comfortable than that from my day."

I smiled at that and inwardly felt amazed that he was handling all of this so well. Then again, he had Nathaniel as his guide.

Mary-Beth, Poppy, and I all ordered our food, and it came out just a few minutes later.

"So, Olin," Mary-Beth asked around a mouthful. "The world's a completely different place. What's the plan?"

Olin looked over at her, frozen for a moment at her blunt question. The air surrounding the table grew heavier. My stomach tightened with the awkwardness.

"I…I do not know," he answered. "Everyone I once cared about is dead. I do not know how this new world works. I hope you all do not mind if I stay with you until I can figure out once more what my place is."

"Our plan is to create a school," Nathaniel said, "where we can train other mages as we find them. We could certainly use your help."

I looked up at Borden, who was glaring darkly at Nathaniel.

I understood it immediately. Nathaniel trusted quickly. Sometimes too quickly.

But I also knew where Nathaniel was coming from. We could use all the help we could get.

"A school?" Olin questioned. "Specifically for witches? Excuse me, mages?"

Nathaniel nodded.

"We need a safe place for those like us to practice," I said, stepping in, because this was my dream, my vision. "There are more of us out there. I know it. We aren't entirely extinct, just hidden, lost. We have a way to test them quickly, to know if they have mage blood. We don't want to flounder anymore. If we can do this properly, if we can teach them in a safe way, just imagine what we can become."

I saw something spark in Olin's eyes. Excitement. Hope.

Finally, he nodded. "Then, that is my plan. I will help you with this school. And maybe someday, we can even find a way to undo what Euan Sandris did."

He looked down at Mary-Beth, who paused the

inhalation of her breakfast. With hope in her eyes as well, she nodded.

"It's settled then," Nathaniel said with a nod.

"We need to get going," my father said just a few moments later, looking at his watch. "The bus will be here in just a few minutes."

We all wolfed down our last few bites and left money on the table. We were all tripping over each other as we scrambled outside with our bags. The bus pulled up right as we ran up to it, and we all piled in.

I scooped up three rocks sitting on the side of the road just before I stepped on. Borden gave me a knowing look.

The bus was crowded. Being the last one on, I watched as the others scattered where there were seats available.

So there was no other option but to sit in the last empty one beside Nathaniel.

He tucked his bag into the overhead bin and automatically reached for mine, stashing it next to his. He extended his hand for me to take the window seat.

My throat felt tight as I sank into the seat, and he sat next to me. Awkwardly, neither of us said anything as the passengers around us settled into their seats, and the bus rolled forward.

"You think we can trust Olin?" I asked, keeping an eye on the back of the man's head. He spoke quietly with my father, who sat across from him, explaining things.

"I'm not sure what other choice we have," Nathaniel said, watching the man as well. "We need information. He knows how to do things we don't. And he hasn't given us any reason to suspect anything."

"It's only been ten hours," I pointed out.

"And it's only been twenty-four with Poppy," Nathaniel countered.

I raised an eyebrow, giving him that.

"Besides, Borden's keeping a close eye on him," Nathaniel said, and both our eyes slid to Borden, who sat two rows behind Olin. He was watching him intently. "I'm pretty sure if he breathes wrong, he'll electrocute him to death."

I believed it. Borden had a short temper and a quick spark. Literally.

I gave a noise of acknowledgment but turned my attention to the rocks in my hand.

"How's the alchemy coming along?" Nathaniel asked, looking down at them.

I swallowed once, but my throat felt dry and tight. I hated that we were this disconnected now, that he didn't even know that I'd gotten control over it. That I'd been making a lot of money off of it.

"Good," I said simply. "I've gotten a good enough grip on it that I'm selling the gold."

Nathaniel's eyes flicked up to me at that, and I couldn't quite read the expression on his face.

"I talked to a realtor not long before we left," I said,

pushing through all of the information. "He gave me an amount he thought the Asteria family would accept. I've sold enough gold that I have half. I plan to sell more while we're here. My plan is to have enough to buy the mansion when we get back to the States."

"That's in two weeks," Nathaniel said. From his tone, I could tell he was shocked. "How much gold are you planning to make while we're here?"

My stomach dropped, because here was another of our problems. I hadn't told him Borden and I hadn't booked return flights yet. "As much as it takes," I said instead, and instantly I felt guilty for not being entirely truthful.

Nathaniel leaned back into his seat, his eyes losing focus as he mulled over what I'd just told him. He was quiet for a solid thirty seconds. "It's actually kind of incredible," he said, surprising me as he looked back at me. "What you can do. Alchemy. You love Asteria House. And you found a way to make it yours."

I couldn't help it as my eyes dropped down to his lips. Then to his hands, covered in scars from his past. "Not just for me," I said quietly. "For you. For all of us. I just want us to have someplace where we feel safe."

I glanced up and saw Nathaniel studying my lips, the same as I had done. He didn't seem ashamed to be caught doing so. We were close, in this small intimate space together, and for just a second, it was easy to forget our problems and live in the way we had before.

"You're the most incredible person I know, Margot," he said softly.

And if he had leaned forward just a little bit more, I would have lost it. I would have thrown every problem out the window, and I would have kissed him. I could have crawled into his lap and wrapped my arms behind his neck. I would have sighed into his mouth and I would have relished his hands on my hips and the points of contact between my legs.

But I didn't do any of that. Because just then, the man in the seat across from Nathaniel leaned over and asked if he knew the time.

So I leaned away, resting my elbow in the window, and watched the landscape as it flew by.

"I never, ever would have dreamed I'd go to Scotland," Nathaniel said.

I had to squeeze my eyes closed for a moment. Nathaniel's voice washed over me with a power that rattled me to my core.

There were so many broken pieces of our future lying scattered around us, I didn't know how to breathe without hurting myself.

"It is pretty incredible," I said, forcing myself to somehow have a normal conversation. "I just wanted to see California, and now I'm in a totally different country."

"Look at that," Nathaniel said, pointing to an old ruin. It wasn't anything more than stones and decaying mortar, but it was magical all the same. "You don't find things like that in America. The length of history here…it astounds me."

I smiled at the excitement I could physically feel rolling off of him. "What's the most fascinating thing about Scottish history that comes to your mind, right now?"

A smirk formed on his face as his eyes met mine. "The Scots never won a battle when they had the larger numbers."

"What?" I asked with a chuckle.

Nathaniel nodded. "All those battles with the English and every one they fought with the advantageous numbers, they couldn't conquer. The Scots fought best when they were the underdogs."

And for the remainder of our bus ride, Nathaniel told me stories of Scottish history, speaking with such detail and knowledge, it was almost hard to believe he wasn't there to witness it all himself.

I listened with rapt attention, laying my head against the seatback. I smiled, and laughed, and was nearly brought to tears as Nathaniel told me stories of lairds and rebels. I could listen to him talk about history all day. And for the remainder of our travels that day, I did.

We might have had our issues when it came to us as a couple, but for now, we were making headway in becoming friends once again.

CHAPTER THREE

The McGregors came from an area in the western region of Scotland called Argyll. It was largely a collection of islands, which made my father's job more challenging. There would be a lot of travel by boat. The McGregors had spread throughout the islands, helping to set up villages and farms.

We would be staying on the island of Inverlagg, which was accessed by a narrow little road that, we'd been told by the bus driver, was frequently washed away by storms at high tide. But it looked stable enough at the moment, so we crossed the road and had no issue getting to the island.

Inverlagg wasn't large, but it was big enough to house a population of fifty-three. They were all farms, spread throughout the green area that took my breath away. There were random rock outcroppings, all covered in green moss, trying to take over everything. The fields were so lush. There were sheep everywhere.

And there was the ocean. I could see it in almost every direction.

We turned down a road, and there was an old house, large and sprawling. It was well taken care of, despite its obvious old age.

The bus stopped, and since the only ones left aboard were our group, we took our time gathering our things and climbing off. Nathaniel handed me my bag, and we all filed off and out into the breezy Scottish air.

I hardly paid any attention to the bed and breakfast as I walked forward. Not when there was that ocean view. And not with that breathtaking reality in front of me.

Out across the water, I could see a *castle*.

It was crumbling into ruins, but still it stood, stone and beautiful.

"That is Castle Sween," my father said as he came to stand beside me with his bags. "Built in the late twelfth century."

"One of the oldest in Scotland," Nathaniel said as he too looked out at the structure.

"You two know a lot about Scottish history, considering neither of you is Scot," Poppy said.

"I forget we only just met," I said with a smile. "My father is a history professor at Alderidge University in the States. And Nathaniel is a history major."

"No need to brag," Poppy teased. "I could tell both of you were smart."

I wanted to laugh because I'd once teased Nathaniel with nearly the same words. Though now, that felt like it was forever ago.

"Come on," Dad said. "Let's get checked in."

And so the seven of us made our way toward the main door as our bus pulled away and headed back to the mainland.

A kind round woman greeted us when we arrived. She introduced herself as Mrs. Bagby, and didn't even seem to mind that we'd brought along two more people than originally planned. She'd just smiled and booked us an extra room. But before we could even make it to our rooms, another woman came walking down the hall.

"Professor Bell?" she asked.

"Janet?" Dad asked with a question.

She simply nodded and extended her hand to shake my father's.

"Margot," Dad said, turning to me, "this is Janet McGregor. She is the other professor working on this study grant."

"Nice to meet you," I said, shaking her hand.

"And you as well," she said in what I was fairly sure was an Australian accent. "Looks like you've brought quite the crowd with you, Arthur."

Dad turned and looked back at what was indeed a

crowd. "Yes, seems I've gained a few spares in the last couple of months."

Janet just smiled, but then turned somber. "I'm really sorry to hear about your wife. Still no leads?"

And instantly my heart slid down to my feet.

It was my mother who had applied for this study grant, to come to the land her ancestors were from, to study them, and her history.

Only, by the time it was approved, she had been missing for nearly four years.

"Thank you," Dad said. "And there is one new possible lead, but we will see."

That lead was the discovery of a book about creating portals.

I *knew* we had our answer about what had happened to her. She'd used magic she couldn't control, and had walked through to somewhere in the world she wasn't familiar.

I had to believe she was still out there somewhere, simply unable to make her way home.

"I'm glad to hear that," Janet said, sounding a little uncomfortable with this heavy situation. "If you want to get settled into your rooms, you and I can get started right away."

"Of course," Dad said, instantly excited once more for this opportunity.

Like good little kids, we'd stayed silent while the

adults talked. But as Janet walked away, I quickly drew out my wand and let it brush her arm as she walked by.

It did not glow blue.

Which made little sense to me, considering somehow we were both related to the same McGregors, who were mages.

But at least we knew.

I didn't miss the surprised looks on my friends' faces when she was gone.

But we moved on, and we all started claiming rooms and roommates.

It was no surprise when I paired up with Mary-Beth. It was the plan from the beginning. Poppy insisted on getting her own room. And like the grumpy old soul he was, Borden informed Nathaniel he could deal with Olin in his room. Borden got his own. And of course, my father had his own, which was all paid for by the grant.

Mary-Beth and I walked into our ground floor room. And it took my breath away when the windows looked out right at the ocean.

"Dibs on the bed closer to the bathroom," Mary-Beth said, setting her bag on it.

"That's fine," I said. I really didn't care. I just walked to the window and stared out at the waves.

I'd grown up, my entire life, within a few hundred yards of the ocean. It had always called to me and I knew it always would. It was one of the reasons I loved Asteria House so much. It was right on the water.

But this ocean felt different. It felt older. It felt a little more magical. It felt deeper.

"You think we'll find them here?" Mary-Beth asked. "The answers we need?"

I shook my head. "I don't know. Borden seems to think so. Nathaniel seems hopeful. But magic has been gone for so long; I just don't know."

Mary-Beth walked up behind me and wrapped her arms around me, laying her head on my shoulder. "It's rotten finding out that I really am broken. But I'm glad to at least have an answer as to why."

I laid my hand over hers, swaying just a little. "I'm so sorry, Mary-Beth. Let's just pray that we can find a solution."

She nodded.

And then there was a knock on the door. It swung open and in popped Nathaniel's head.

"Let's get going," he said. "We only have fourteen days. Don't want to waste any of them."

I smiled, because even though I was exhausted and really wanted a nap, he was right. Borden and I might not only have fourteen days, but the rest of our group did.

We had called ahead of time, and the owners of the bed and breakfast had procured bicycles for our group. So the lot of us met out front, grabbed them, and together, we pointed toward the far end of the island.

It spoke to the magic of our surroundings. Even

though there were six of us, hardly a word was spoken as we rode across the island. Each of us soaked up our surroundings. We all took it in in silence, watching the rolling land. Taking in the simple dirt roads. The fields of sheep. The endless views of the ocean.

This island was old. I could tell that. Each of the homes were made of stone with at least one chimney rising from it. While Harrington was old, multiple centuries, and Boston even older, this architecture spoke of centuries of elder age.

I watched Nathaniel as we rode in silence. I'd never seen so much peace on his face. So much fascination. He loved history. He loved age. And he was walking among it in a way he never expected to be able to do. He'd thanked Mary-Beth profusely, over and over since we landed. She'd been ridiculous about it, of course, making jokes about him spending the rest of his life paying her back, which he offered to do. But she'd just rolled her eyes and teased him more.

Watching Nathaniel, I was happy too. I wanted him to be happy. I wanted him to feel at peace. Neither of us had felt much of that since we'd broken up.

For a little while, I felt it then.

We turned down another road, and there was a sign, pointing the way to our destination.

Inverlagg Library.

Really, it was little more than a crumbling barn with stained glass windows. But it was charming and beautiful all the same. We each parked our bikes to the side of it, and one by one, we filed inside.

The poor little librarian startled fiercely when we walked in, her eyes going wide.

"You must be the group Mrs. Bagby warned me about," the woman said.

Warned. I wanted to laugh at that.

"Yes," Nathaniel said, slipping into his easy professional mode he'd acquired from three years of work in Alderidge's library. "My name is Nathaniel Nightingale. These are my friends."

"We're in the area doing research on my ancestors, the McGregors," I said, stepping up to his side, which felt like the most natural thing in the world to do. "I hope you don't mind us taking a look through your little library."

"That's what it's here for," the woman, who hadn't introduced herself, said. "Let me know if you'd like to borrow anything."

And with that, she went back to her task of reading a romance novel with a very scandalous cover.

Nathaniel and I just shared a snickering look, then stepped further into the library.

Quietly, Nathaniel set to explaining our wands to Poppy and Olin, while the rest of us, me, Borden, and Mary-Beth, immediately set to testing the books on the shelves.

It was quite the assortment of books. Some were

brand new, others looked ancient. I couldn't find any rhyme or reason to the organization. Fiction was mixed with non-fiction. There were children's books stuffed in with the science-fiction. As far as I could tell, they'd just been crammed into whatever empty space there was on the shelf.

I could only imagine how it was killing Nathaniel on the inside.

I finished one row of books, and moved on to the next.

"This really works?" Poppy asked as she came to my side. "You just touch the pencils to the spines and they change?"

"Remember what I showed you before?" I asked, thinking back on how I'd shown her at the airport. Duplicating it, I extended my gloved hand toward her and poked her bare arm. Instantly, it glowed blue. She laughed in delight. "It does the same with magical books."

She shook her head. "I still can't believe this is real. What am I supposed to do with my life now? I'm supposed to go back to work in three days. But now…" She shook her head. "I don't know how I'm just supposed to go back to my normal job when I know what you all are doing."

"You can join us," I said, looking back at her. "In fact, I really, really hope you will. We need all of us. Together. Learning and discovering. We were nearly hunted out of extinction once. What few of us are left need to stick together."

"It's not exactly simple though, you know," she said, following me as I walked along the shelves, testing the books. "To just walk away from the only life I've known. To give up my job and commit to being a full-time mage. I mean, how am I supposed to support myself if I join you all?"

I paused and thought about it. How was she supposed to do it? I had alchemy. Borden and Mary-Beth were rich on their own. Nathaniel had his scholarship. But where did that leave Poppy?

"I don't know," I answered honestly. "But I do know that we can figure something out. I will do whatever I can to keep us all together. That's a promise, if you're willing to stick with us."

Poppy held my eyes for a long moment. "You're a good person," she said. "I hardly even know you, Margot, but I can already tell. I believe you when you say that."

I nodded. "Nathaniel is obsessed with our history. Borden wants to know the extent of what we can do. Mary-Beth wants to unlock her magic. But I just want us all together. To take care of us and to make sure we're safe. It's all I really care about. Gathering us all together."

"Aren't you quite the little mother hen?" Poppy teased. I smiled in return. "And I wonder what my place in all of this is going to be. Maybe I can become Poppy, the recruiter. I can travel all around the world with my job, finding and collecting all of the lost mages."

I raised an eyebrow. "That's an interesting idea. You just may be on to something there, Poppy."

I'd reached the end of my section and now stood with my arms folded while the others finished their areas. By this point, I was getting used to disappointment at not finding anything. It was just something we had to come to accept, that we wouldn't always find what we were looking for. It had been too much time, and not all mages were going to bother writing down instruction books.

One by one, I watched as my fellow mages came to the end of their sections, and one by one, none of them found any magical books.

Borden came to stand beside me as he finished his section, his lips set thin with disappointment.

Mary-Beth finished up, looking bummed out.

And then Nathaniel finished up, Olin silently watching by his side.

"I really thought we'd find something here," Mary-Beth said. "I just kind of figured Europe was going to be overflowing with magical shit, you know?"

We all laughed, but it was a small, controlled one, because each of us was disappointed.

Nathaniel made his way to the librarian again, who looked up at him from over the top of her reading glasses.

"Maybe you can help us," he said. "See, we're here on

a special project. I'm a history major, and have always had a bit of a fascination with the witch hunts in Europe."

The woman didn't even bother trying to hide her eye roll.

"And my friend here," Nathaniel didn't specify which of us, "is the descendant of someone killed in one of those witch hunts. I was wondering if you knew where we might get some more information on what happened during those events."

The woman sighed as she got to her feet and leaned forward on her desk. "If it's witches you're after, you might talk to Agnes McGregor."

Instantly, my stomach jumped up into my throat. McGregor.

"She's a little crazy in the head if you ask me," the librarian continued. "But she's been obsessed with the history of witch hunts as well. She knows all about that dark side of our history."

Nathaniel looked over at me, his eyes bright with excitement. "And where can I find Agnes McGregor?" he asked.

The woman signed and turned to a map hung on the wall. "She lives on that tiny island off the north coast." She pointed to a small island just detached from Inverlagg on the north side. This island wasn't large, that one was far smaller. "Nothing much left there but herself and her dogs. But she'll talk to you, talk you to death if you're willin' to listen."

"And how do we get there?" Borden asked.

"I imagine you'll want to find a boat, unless you feel like testing your swimming lungs," she said as if Borden were stupid.

Annoyed at the woman, I looked away, barely resisting an eye roll myself.

"Thank you for your help," Nathaniel offered, always too polite.

The lot of us filed out of the library and back to our bikes.

"You think this woman really knows anything?" I asked to the general group as I kicked up my kickstand, and we all hopped onto our bikes, pointed back in the direction of the bed and breakfast.

"It's possible," Nathaniel said. "She's a direct McGregor. Has to originate from the same line. And she lives in the right region."

"If she's being called crazy, it's likely for a reason," Borden said. "She may seem odd to others, but if she's just talking about things they can't understand…"

"It's likely she's telling the truth, just not what's normal for others," Olin added.

I looked up into the sky. The sun was aiming for the west horizon. A few more hours, and it would be dark.

"Let's see what we can do about securing a boat for tomorrow," I said. "We'll plan to leave first thing in the morning."

In the meantime, Borden and I had some business to take care of.

We weren't trying to be secretive, but it felt weird explaining to everyone that I was doing alchemy and, largely out of a sense of safety and security, Borden was coming with me. So, when we got back to the bed and breakfast, we made excuses. And then Borden and I got on our bikes and headed for the road, back to the main island, where we'd seen a jeweler.

"So, what do you think of Scotland so far?" Borden asked as we peddled and headed across the road surrounded by ocean.

"It's really beautiful," I answered, feeling myself relax just a bit. Somehow, in recent months, Borden brought that out in me. "And the lead with Agnes has me hopeful. What do you think?"

Borden shrugged, and I took a moment to observe him. His hair had grown a little longer. He hadn't bothered to cut it since Dean Lowell expelled us from Alderidge. His eyes were broody, and his lips set in a serious line.

Borden really was an attractive man. With broad shoulders and a fit body, he could get any girl he wanted.

But that wasn't why I was evaluating him.

"I've been to Scotland before," he said. "Dad liked to come golfing in the motherland. And it's not raining, which is always a positive. I've been here before where it rained every single day for a week."

That didn't surprise me. Even now, I could see dark clouds out on the horizon. But in this moment, they stayed far enough away that I wasn't concerned.

"The library was disappointing," Borden admitted. "I really thought we'd find things. That we'd be finding magical help all over the place. But I have to be realistic. The mages made up a fractional portion of the population. So I guess we just count ourselves lucky we have the lead with Agnes."

I had to agree.

We turned right down a road and found ourselves in a little village. There were several restaurants and half a dozen shops that had me itching to grab my purse. There was a church and a bank. And there in the middle of them all, was the jeweler.

It wasn't as easy as it was in America. This man asked a lot more questions and seemed far more suspicious as to why a couple of young adults were in possession of so much raw gold. But we lied and told a convincing story that slowly persuaded the man that nothing was afoul. And in the end, I walked out of there with an envelope full of cash.

We took our time getting back to the bed and breakfast. We got some food to go, and just after we crossed the road back onto Inverlagg, we stopped at the beach and ate.

"What if we find everything we need here?" Borden asked after swallowing a massive bite. "What if we get all of our answers and find all of the resources we need here, in Scotland, or somewhere in Europe? Would you ever consider setting up the school here?"

I looked over at Borden and finished my bite as I studied him. "Why are you so anxious to get out of Harrington?"

I could tell I'd gotten it right when his eyes met mine. I saw something sad and terrible there. Something regretful and a little haunted.

"You're very observant, you know that, Margot Bell?"

I offered a sad little smile but didn't say anything.

Borden looked out at the water. "I made a lot of mistakes in Harrington. I went to Alderidge determined to make my father proud and to live up to the Stewart legacy. Then I found I hated everything about my family's culture and everything to do with high society. But the anger gave me access to my powers, and so I sank in deeper and deeper with the Society Boys. I became someone I hated. I did some truly atrocious things. My life got better when you and Nathaniel came into the picture. But still, everything I knew fell apart."

I reached over and took Borden's hand, giving it a supportive squeeze.

"So I guess I'm anxious to move on with my life," he said, looking down at our hands. "I just want to start over and be the person I'm discovering. And Harrington is full of ghosts that prevent me from doing that."

"We can't let the past contaminate the future," I said,

rubbing my thumb over the back of his hand. "And you have to learn to forgive. Not just others, but yourself. Especially yourself. You didn't know then. And now you do. So do yourself a favor. Forget all those things about yourself, those things in Harrington, and just live in the moment."

Borden met my eyes again, and we stared at each other. "You're really wise. Did you know that?" he said quietly, expanding his earlier comment.

I sensed the moment getting too heavy and too deep. So I laughed and tossed sand at him. "Help me find some rocks, Stewart heir."

And it worked. The weight and knot in my stomach disappeared. Borden laughed, and things went back to normal.

We found four smaller rocks. One by one, I used my alchemy to transform them into gold, and then we went back to the bed and breakfast.

CHAPTER FOUR

I noticed something the next morning as we rode our bikes down to the dock and waited for the boat we chartered.

Nathaniel wouldn't look me in the eye.

He wouldn't look at Borden either.

And Mary-Beth was watching Borden and me with suspicion.

I hated it.

I hated that there was any ounce of complication to this.

I hated that I felt like I had to explain.

I hated that it couldn't just be comfortable, that we couldn't just be friends without everyone else thinking there was something going on.

There wasn't anything going on. We were just friends.

And I didn't want to have to feel like I had to explain that.

So I ignored it instead.

Which was probably a very bad idea.

The boat arrived, and we all climbed aboard. And I forgot all my troubles as the boat pulled away from the dock, and we headed out over the ocean.

I had grown up my entire life within a few hundred yards of the ocean, yet I could count the number of times I'd been on a boat on one hand. Dad had spent a lot of his years as a youth out on a boat with his father, fishing and exploring. But when he was fourteen years old, they'd gotten into a boat accident.

Dad was able to swim back to shore. But his father never made it back, and it took them four days to recover his body.

Dad had never been on a boat since.

I never forgot that story. It was a part of my family history, so I had always had a respect for the ocean, and I had kept my distance from boats, other than the few times a friend had invited me to go out with them.

But being out here on this boat, I closed my eyes for a few seconds, and lived in the moment.

The feel of the wind on my face was exhilarating. The ocean air smelled clean and fresh. The sound of the spray was hypnotizing.

I told myself to appreciate every magical moment here in Scotland.

And it was all over in five minutes. The tiny island really was close to the shore of Inverlagg, and we arrived just a few short minutes after we left.

There was a dock stretching out from the shore, and moored there was an old boat that didn't look particularly seaworthy to me. But we docked, and each of us climbed out. The captain had agreed to wait ten minutes, and if we didn't come right back out, he would leave and return a few hours later.

Nervous, I looked ahead as we walked down the dock.

Immediately, I could see a smaller house. It was stone, much like the others in the region. Plants were growing up the side of it, consuming the building slowly. There was a massive garden to the south of the house, where I could see rows and rows of produce beginning to spring from the ground. To the north of the house, there was a field with a dozen sheep.

And the moment we stepped foot off of the dock onto the dirt path, a pack of dogs started barking, and soon ran up to us.

Olin stepped behind Mary-Beth, using her as a shield. Mary-Beth also took a nervous step backward. But Poppy and Nathaniel just smiled, extending their hands out for the dogs to sniff.

They weren't vicious. Within a few moments, they were wagging their tails and licking Poppy and Nathaniel's hands.

"Oy!" a voice yelled from up by the house. A female voice then yelled a slew of words in what I thought was Gaelic.

And then a moment later, she stepped into view, and stood frozen when she saw our group.

She had the kind of hair that was fading from blonde to gray. It had been pulled up in a bun at the back of her head, but now there were wisps of it going everywhere. She wore a skirt that seemed a little out of time, and a white shirt that buttoned up the front.

She seemed oddly…timeless. Like she could be from this century or the last as easy as breathing.

"We're really sorry to just intrude like this," I said, stepping forward. "We couldn't find a phone number to reach you, and we couldn't think of any other way to get in touch."

She folded her arms over her middle and looked at us with absolute distrust. "What is your business coming here?"

I looked back at my group, but specifically at Nathaniel. He was always the one that was the best at this.

"We're doing some research on the McGregor family," he said, stepping forward. "Some rather…specific research."

Agnes continued to eye us for several long moments. "And why are you so interested in my family line?"

"Because both of us are descendants of Mare

McGregor," I said, indicating myself and Mary-Beth, "who moved to America from Scotland in 1690."

At that, Agnes raised her eyebrows and stood just a little straighter.

"Well, if you're kin, perhaps you should come inside and have a cuppa."

She didn't wait for us to respond. She turned and walked back toward the house.

We glanced at each other, then hurried along to go catch up with her.

The gardening around the house was beautiful. All the flowers were just beginning to bloom, and it smelled like heaven. The dogs excitedly swarmed around us, barking happily at the company.

I stopped when I stepped inside, stunned into silence.

It was the coziest place I'd ever seen. It was stuffed to the brim with things. The ceilings were low. There were rugs everywhere. A fire was glowing, and the place was warm and smelled like bread.

It was the kind of place you wanted to curl up in with a blanket and just sit and read a book or two.

Realizing I was blocking the doorway, I walked further in, and went to watch Agnes bustling in the kitchen, putting on a pot to boil.

"I hope the house isn't too much a mess," she said. "Don't get much company around here."

"You're home is beautiful," I said, and I truly meant

it. "Thank you for inviting us in. Again, we're sorry to just barge in on you like this."

She looked over her shoulder and studied me for a second, as if she could read my true intentions off of my skin.

"Can I help you with that?" Poppy said, stepping forward when Agnes turned for the loaf of bread she turned out of a pan.

"So, you're not all American?" she asked, handing Poppy the knife while she turned to a shelf and pulled down a jar of homemade jam.

"No, ma'am," Olin said in his undeniable English accent.

She just glared at him, and I smiled, thinking of all the history between the two countries Nathaniel had told me about.

"It's just those two," I said, noting that Borden and Nathaniel were making themselves comfortable and looking around her little home. "The rest of us are from the States."

"But it's just you two that are of McGregor blood?" she asked as she put out cups. There were only six, and then cupboard was bare.

"Yep," Mary-Beth said, not waiting to officially be served. She grabbed a slice of bread from in front of Poppy, who smacked her hand with the flat part of the knife. "But we don't like to leave these other bozos out of the fun. They're good for more than they look."

At that, Agnes raised an eyebrow again and looked around at the whole of our group.

"You have quite the collection of books," Nathaniel said from the living room. "How do you get most of them?"

Agnes carried the pot and the stack of chipped cups to the table and set them down. "I travel every now and then. I get them on those occasions."

"Some of them look quite old," Borden said. "I imagine you might have inherited a few."

She looked at him, again, like she was trying to read all of his truths from his face. "A few."

I came to sit at the table, and Mary-Beth sat across from me. One by one, they all came to sit, and Agnes began pouring tea into the cups she had.

"Can I ask?" I said, looking up at her. "Why do you live out here on this little island, all by yourself?"

She finished and set sugar and cream on the table. "I was born here, same as my mother. It's easier living in separation than persecution."

I met Nathaniel's eyes, and my certainty grew more confident.

"Agnes, we're here trying to learn about the McGregors who were killed in the witch trials," Borden said, cutting right to the throat of it all. "Margot and Mary-Beth's ancestor was killed in the States, but we know there were other McGregors accused here in Scotland."

Agnes stood straight, and I could see all the defenses going up in her, flashing across her face. "If you're here to point fingers and make fun of me, I'll kindly ask you to leave right now."

My throat was tight, and there were knots in my stomach.

But Borden just shook his head. "That isn't my goal, Miss McGregor. See, my name is Borden Stewart, and I had an ancestor who was also killed for being a witch."

Something sparked to life in Agnes' eyes as she looked at Borden.

"And mine, William Nightingale, was also killed for being a witch," Nathaniel piped up.

"My grandmother was burned at the stake," Olin said, divulging new information.

"All…all of you?" Agnes asked in a breath, her eyes flicking to every one of us.

We each just nodded, and I could see her trust and her excitement growing by the second.

"I…I have met other locked, but never any who were aware of their history," she said in a breath as she finally sat down at the head of the table.

Shared glances were cast around the table. And then I looked back at Agnes. "You've met other locked mages—witches—who didn't know what they were?"

Agnes nodded.

"Have you ever met one who was not locked, and knew what they were?" I asked in a breath.

"No, never," Agnes answered, her eyes gleaming with excitement.

I swallowed once and nodded.

We were about to change so much in this woman's world.

I focused on the empty pot on the table, and I asked it to rise. Immediately, it lifted into the air.

Nathaniel sent a stack of paper on a shelf flying into the air, every one of them folding into a crane.

Borden sent a surge of electricity through the lights, causing them to flicker and surge brighter.

Agnes sucked in a shocked breath. She looked around at it all, taking in hard pulls, her eyes wide, blinking too much.

"You…" she breathed. "You can still do magic."

I let the pot lower back to the table. Nathaniel unfolded his cranes and returned them to the pile. Borden released the lights, and they went back to normal.

Agnes stared at the lot of us, blinking and shaking her head in disbelief. "I thought everyone who knew was gone. That they had all died out. And now…here you are, showing up at my house. Six of you, magic users."

Mary-Beth shook her head. "Five. Not quite all of us were so lucky."

Still, Agnes gaped, seemingly at a loss for words.

"Please, Miss McGregor," Nathaniel said, filling the silence. "We've only just learned about ourselves within the last ten months. We know very little. What can you share with us?"

She sucked in an excited breath, and in a whirlwind, she stood and went to a row of bookshelves. "The last McGregor who could still do magic, was Lokin McGregor." She grabbed one book and brought it back to the table. She opened it to somewhere near the beginning and laid it in front of us all. We found it was a family tree, with handwritten names spread throughout in an organized manner. "Just after he and his wife, a non-magic woman, married, magic was locked."

My heart started beating, faster and faster as she began sharing information with us.

"He kept his magic, but every child he had could not access it."

"What are these empty spaces?" Nathaniel asked, pointing to two empty lines.

"We know Lokin had five children," Agnes said as she paced. "My line comes through Gilbert. And then there was Androe and Jeane. I haven't been able to find record of the names of those other two children."

"Mare," Mary-Beth and I said at the exact same time.

"One of them was Mare," I said. "She's the one who went to America and was killed for being a witch."

"My family has a lot of family history records," Mary-Beth said. "I don't have them with me now, but I can mail you a copy when I get back to the States."

Agnes nodded happily, but I could see the wheels in

her brain running a million miles a minute. "That…that means not all of Lokin's children were locked. If this Mare was killed for being a witch…"

"She had full access to her magic," I filled in. "I have her journal."

For which, I should be ashamed. I hadn't read it yet, other than a little skimming. After seeing that vision with Mary-Beth in Salem, I was scared.

"What a treasure," Agnes breathed. "I would very much love to see it. Witches in America. I had no idea any of that hullabaloo was real."

"There was another true witch killed there too," Nathaniel pointed out. "So far, we haven't found any evidence of her posterity having lived on."

Agnes shook her head. I could only imagine how overwhelming this must be. She's spent her life learning about her family history, and here we were, living proof she wasn't crazy.

"I assume none of you have yet found the key to unlocking magic?" she asked cautiously. Her eyes rose up to meet Mary-Beth's.

"No," I said. "I'm sorry. But like I said, we're still right at the beginning of this. We still are uncovering truths and treasures every single day. So, I'm hopeful, that someday…" I trailed off as I met my friend's eyes, knowing how much she hoped and wished.

Agnes simply nodded. "Well, tell me what you do know, and perhaps I can fill in some holes."

. . .

WE SPENT HOURS TALKING. We shared our knowledge. Olin nearly made the poor woman faint when he told her about himself. We painted the picture of what we knew. And Agnes shared her knowledge of our family's history.

The McGregors were a strong clan, but they were hot-headed and willing to take on sometimes impossible things. They often fought with the other clans, and from Agnes' stories, they often put themselves at risk in exposing their abilities because of their tempers. People died. There was distrust and gossip about the family.

But they managed to stay out of the crosshairs of the witch hunts that ran through Scotland. And then it came to Lokin McGregor, magic was locked, and that was the end of the mage history in our family line.

In the afternoon, we all found ourselves curled up in the living room, and the stories shifted away from family history.

"There was once an archive," Agnes said as she tucked her feet up underneath her and took a sip from her cup. "It's talked about in several journals. Throughout the years, it was moved in order to protect it."

"An archive," Nathaniel asked, his voice instantly intrigued. "How do you mean?"

"It was a library," she explained, meeting his eyes. "A collection of all the mage wisdom from the area. And there were the keepers—mages who had knowledge passed down to them, knowledge too dangerous to keep a written record of."

The hair on the back of my arms stood on end at the thought of it all. An entire library, wise teachers who held the world's knowledge of magic, secret magic too dangerous to keep a written record of.

"What happened to it?" Poppy asked.

Agnes looked over at her. "It disappeared a year before Euan Sandris locked magic. He'd been looking for it for a few years. Said he would destroy it, so its evils could be kept from the world. So the keepers fled with the archive."

"And no one knows where they went?" Olin asked.

Agnes shook her head. "No one heard from the Keepers ever again. They disappeared, and took the majority of the world's knowledge of magic with them."

"Do you think it was destroyed?" Borden asked.

"I don't believe so," Agnes said, taking another sip. "Those men and women were the best the world had ever seen. It would have taken a lot to take them out and destroy what they were protecting."

"So, what do you think happened to the archive?" Olin asked.

She looked over at him. "I think they hid it. And I think they used magic to do it. They knew there would be others like Sandris, and they knew the knowledge within that archive would give the bad people in this world the ability to do even worse things. So I think they hid the archive and protected it so the wrong hands would never get on it."

"But where?" Olin asked. "Where do you think they would hide such a treasure trove?"

Agnes shrugged. "In all my years, my lifetime of research, I have never found any clues."

"Doesn't that kind of make them just the same as Sandris?" Borden asked. "Sandris was trying to lock everyone out of their magic. Didn't the Keepers do the same thing by taking away the archive?"

"Don't think I haven't thought the same thing," Agnes said. "And I'm not alone. For years, the magical world was angry with the Keepers for hiding away the archive. Perhaps there was a solution within it that could unlock magic again. And the mages couldn't defend themselves well, because they did not know how. And look what happened within a few decades. Witches were nearly hunted to extinction, and most were so afraid of the world they decided to forget about their magic. Look at the world today. As far as I know, you lot are the only ones in the world who can still practice. You all are a miracle as far as I'm concerned. You came from America, where there were very, very few witches. And look what you can do. What you've accomplished. And you're little more than teenagers."

"Finding out you can do real magic is fairly motivating," Borden said.

Agnes just chuckled.

Just then, there was the sound of a horn, rippling out over the ocean.

Nathaniel looked down at his watch. "That would be our boat."

Panic surged in my throat. We had so much more to learn. I had so many more questions to ask.

"Can we come back?" I blurted out. "We still have so much we need to learn. We have so many questions to ask."

"Please do," Agnes said as she stood, and we started heading for the door. "I have a few more questions to ask myself."

"We'll return tomorrow," Borden stated. "Around the same time, if that's alright?"

Agnes nodded and followed us out to the grass. We each waved to her as we set off down the dock and climbed aboard the boat.

We made arrangements for the captain to pick us up again tomorrow and drop us off here.

"That was amazing," I said as I walked to the side of the boat. I folded my arms and leaned on the edge, looking out at the splashing waves.

"I don't think we could have possibly hoped for a better outcome," Borden said as he sat in the seat beside me. "A historian. Of mages." He shook his head. "Never in my wildest dreams would I have guessed one existed."

I smiled and nodded. And for the first time since I got on that plane back in Boston, I started to feel hope.

Hope that we might really be able to do this. That we might find what we needed while here in Europe.

The others were excitedly chatting behind me, going over the exciting revelations of the day. But I just stayed at the edge of the boat, letting myself be content and ridiculously happy that something had worked out, for once.

We reached the dock and disembarked. Each of our stomachs were growling ravenously, and when Nathaniel told us it was time for dinner to be served, we peddled as fast as we could back to the bed and breakfast.

We walked in just as Dad and Janet sat down to eat at the long table with Mrs. Bagby. With a smile and the shake of her head, she returned to the kitchen to get our plates.

"How was your excursion?" Dad asked as I sat down next to him. He leaned over and pressed a quick kiss to my cheek.

"Couldn't have gone better," I said, smiling, wishing with everything inside of me that Janet wasn't here, and that Mrs. Bagby wasn't walking back in with our dinners, so I could talk freely.

"Are you being serious?" he asked, his eyes widening just a little.

I nodded, unable to contain the wide smile on my face. "I'll tell you all about it later. How was your day?"

"Very informative," he said. "Did you know that the McGregors once had a castle on this very island? And that it was torn down by a warring clan just five years later?"

Now it was my turn to be surprised. My eyes widened, but I didn't even get a chance to say anything, because Nathaniel launched into a volley of questions.

If I were being honest, I really wasn't interested in the McGregor history, outside of mage studies. So I started tuning the two of them out and turned back to the rest of the company at the table.

"I was thinking," Poppy said. "I'm taking all of my vacation time next week. I've got two more days off. So that's nine days. And from what I hear, you all are only here for about that long anyway. Perhaps you could teach me some things in the next few days?"

Instantly, my heart sank and I felt awful. "Of course, Poppy," I said. "I'm so sorry, I've been so wrapped up in everything going on here I kind of forgot that you don't know everything we do."

"None of us know as much as you two do," Mary-Beth pointed out. "That's what happens when you get kicked out of school and get to study full time."

Borden and I looked at each other, and I marveled. Because even though it was only a few days ago, our time together, studying magic full time, felt like months ago. Suddenly, I kind of missed it. Easy hours at my house, or Asteria House, practicing and learning. Making jokes and talking about what to expect in Europe.

Borden smiled a little, and I wondered if he was thinking about the same thing.

I looked back at Poppy. "Let's get up early in the morning, and we can work on some things."

"I would love to join, if you don't mind," Olin spoke up.

"Of course," I said, smiling with a nod. "What do you say, Borden? You up for an early morning training session?"

He smiled. "I'm not the one who sleeps in every day it's allowed. I'm up every morning at the same time."

I chuckled, thinking how rigid and organized he always was. "It sounds like a plan then. We'll get started at seven."

I turned to look at the others, and my stomach sank when Nathaniel sat there with a serious look on his face. His eyes flicked from Borden to me and back to Borden. Then, he looked down at his plate and continued to eat in silence.

CHAPTER FIVE

Late that night, I finished my shower and walked back to my room, my hair dripping wet. I paused just before turning into my room when I saw Borden standing in the hall, leaning against the wall.

"What are you doing out here?" I asked, rubbing the towel through my hair.

"There was a leak in the ceiling of my room," Borden said. "Mrs. Bagby has a repairman in there. Should be done in a few minutes."

I nodded. "You want to come in my room for now?"

And of course—*of course*—Nathaniel walked out into the hall just then, hearing what I'd just said.

He looked between the two of us, his lips set in a thin line. But he didn't say anything, and that was the problem. I wanted him to yell and ask questions and get a little upset. But he said nothing. He just walked down the hall, his towel over his shoulder, and shut the door to the bathroom.

I felt sick.

I didn't want things to be this way.

So tomorrow, I would find my chance. I would get Nathaniel alone, and I would put the record straight.

"Night, Borden," I said, my voice hoarse.

"Night, Margot," he said, and I knew I heard something a little tragic and sorrowful in his voice as I stepped into my room and shut the door behind me.

Mary-Beth was already sound asleep when I walked in. From her bed, closest to the bathroom, she snored. I smiled at her. She slept like a starfish, sprawled out and taking up every inch of the bed. Her poor future husband, whoever he might be. He was going to end up on the floor every night.

I brushed my hair and then my teeth. And then, turning out the lamp, I crawled beneath the covers and stared up at the ceiling.

Everything felt a little overwhelming right then. We had the entirety of Europe to search for traces of magic. And I knew we wouldn't get so lucky next time and find a mage historian to ask all of our questions.

And then this drama with Nathaniel and Borden.

I hardly even wanted to think about it, but then again, I knew that wasn't how an adult would handle the situation.

I huffed and rolled over, pulling the blankets tight around my chin.

But the sound of voices pulled me back fully awake.

Nathaniel's room was right next to mine and Mary-Beth's. And from it, I could hear him…and Borden.

"What proof are you basing this off of?" Borden asked, and I knew him well enough now that I could tell he was using every ounce of self-restraint to keep himself calm.

"Don't try and play stupid with me, Borden," Nathaniel said. For the first time ever, I heard a faint trace of that danger he'd told me about. "You two have spent so much time together recently. It's obvious she trusts you. She's said so herself, that she can be who she is in a way she can't be around me. I just want the truth."

During their pause, I realized just how hard my heart was pounding in my ears. My stomach was in knots, and I felt like I could throw up.

"You shouldn't even have to ask," Borden said, his tone lower and calmer. "You say you love her, and you say you trust her. So you shouldn't have to ask."

"But I am," Nathaniel said, and I heard him breaking. "Because she's said nothing has happened, but I've still seen what I've seen between the two of you. I've still seen the weight lift off her shoulders when she's around you. And I've seen the way you look at her."

For just a second, my heart stopped.

And I knew. I had to face it.

"So I am asking," Nathaniel said. "Did anything happen between you and Margot before we ended things?"

I squeezed my eyes tighter, trying to eliminate the moisture trying to pool in them.

I hated this. I hated it.

But he wasn't being unfounded.

"I'm telling you, Nathaniel," Borden responded. "Nothing has happened between Margot and I."

There was another beat. And I could only imagine the weight in that room, hanging over them like a physical thing.

"But you have feelings for her." Nathaniel said it as a statement.

There was another full, heavy pause. "Yes."

And my stomach disappeared entirely.

I shouldn't have been surprised. I shouldn't have been shocked.

I'd seen the small glances Borden had cast in my direction. I had to appreciate that he'd come with me, every single time, without hesitation, when I'd asked him to come sell the gold.

We naturally got along in a way I never would have expected. We had some core things in common.

So I shouldn't have been surprised.

And if I were being honest with myself, I wasn't. I'd seen it all along. I'd felt our natural chemistry.

But I'd been ignoring it. Denying it. Because I was

still in love with Nathaniel, and I had no intention of letting our future slip out of our fingers.

"And what do you plan to do about those feelings?" Nathaniel asked.

I held my breath, waiting for the answer.

"It doesn't matter," Borden said, and I wished I could see the expression on his face. "What matters is what are you going to do about it, knowing you aren't the only one who will do anything for Margot."

I waited several moments, but I heard nothing else, until there was the click of a door, and I heard footsteps walking across the hall.

My heart hammered in my chest. Emotions made my throat tight.

I rolled over on my back, and I stared up at the ceiling without really seeing it.

Now I knew. I knew Borden had feelings for me. I knew the time I was spending with him was hurting Nathaniel.

So what was I going to do about it?

CHAPTER SIX

I SLEPT A TOTAL OF ONE HOUR. MIDNIGHT CAME AND went. I said hello to three AM. And finally, around four, I fell into a restless fit of dreams.

Finally, I got out of bed at five and quietly got dressed so I wouldn't wake Mary-Beth. I went outside for a run. I'd never been much of a runner, but I needed to let off steam and work through some things in my head.

I got ready when I got back, and by then, we were all headed to the dining room for breakfast.

We ate. Then we rode our bikes down the beach, to where it was isolated, and no one could see us.

I taught the lesson that day. Really, Nathaniel or Borden could have helped me, but I needed some separation, so I took the reins. I went through it all, everything I knew about levitation. Poppy picked it up slowly. Olin had already known some elements of levitation, but his abilities were shaky at best.

I was starting to realize he didn't know as much as we'd hoped. He'd come from the year 1656 after all. There were few books back then, and even if there were, not everyone could read or write. So much of what the mages knew had to be passed down through words and in-person teaching.

Maybe Borden was wrong. Maybe we weren't going to find as much as we'd hoped for here in Europe.

The tight knot in my chest did not loosen as the day progressed. I was trapped in my own head, going through all of the negative that was going on in my life.

Knowing we might fail. Remembering what had happened last night.

I made a special effort not to make eye contact with Nathaniel or Borden all morning. When we finished our training session and headed for the dock, I kept to myself on the boat.

And I didn't pause for anyone as we walked up the dock to where Agnes was standing outside with her dogs, waiting for us.

"Glad you came back," she said, smiling. "Though, it doesn't look like you will be able to stay so long today."

"Why's that?" I asked in confusion.

She looked out over the ocean. "Storm's coming."

I looked out as well, but all I saw was clear blue skies with a few fluffy white clouds out in the distance.

But I didn't say anything. I wasn't from this area. What did I know?

"Come on in," she said, nodding her head toward the house as our entire group made their way up the path.

We stepped into her cottage, and again, I couldn't help but smile. It was exactly the kind of space I would expect when talking about history and magic.

"I was thinking about it this morning," I said as we all made our way inside. "People weren't widely educated on how to read and write until the turn of *this* century, the nineteen hundreds. So really, there wouldn't be many books created. Or even journals kept."

Agnes set out tea again, and her eyes rose to meet mine. "You're right on that. And even the ones that were created, they've been lost or destroyed or fallen apart. Or disappeared with the archive."

"So, you don't have to answer this question, but how many books do you even have?" Nathaniel asked, and I could hear the disappointment in his words.

She looked up at him, and still I saw hesitance in her eyes, and I couldn't blame her one bit. She had only known us for one day, and this was her life's work. Her most prized possessions.

"Not many," she admitted without giving details.

Collectively, I heard sighs of frustration.

"Still," I said, cutting them off, trying to keep their spirits up and politeness front and center considering we were her guests. "We appreciate anything and everything you can share with us."

She nodded, sensing the frustration with wary eyes.

"Agnes," I said, settling in at the table, Poppy at my side, Olin beside her. "I wonder. Have you ever heard of portal magic? The ability to open up…doors, if you will, and instantly travel to another part of the world?"

She poured her tea and mixed in some sugar. "I've read it talked about. Briefly, and most of it is theoretical. But there was a book, a few years ago, that I was trying to buy at auction. I was outbid though. So, I think so. But I cannot tell you for sure."

I didn't know whether to laugh or cry.

"What?" Agnes asked, her eyes widening a bit. "Why is that look on your face?"

I found my throat tight and the words stuck behind my lips.

"Her mother won a few books at auction a few years back," Borden spoke up when I couldn't. "One was sealed until it wasn't. And the other was about portals."

"Her mother disappeared after that," Nathaniel continued to explain. "We believed she performed the magic in the book and walked through to a different area in the world. Our theory is that she hasn't been able to make it back home yet."

Still unable to form words, I reached for the bag at my feet and pulled the very book out.

Agnes' eyes widened at the sight of it.

I handed it to her, and she took it cautiously.

"None of us dare try it," I said around a thick throat. "She's been missing for four years and still hasn't made her way back. So far, it's the only magic we don't know if we can control."

Agnes ran her fingers over the pages with such reverence. "I'm so sorry to hear that, Margot. Unfortunately, there is little way more to test magic. We experiment with our own lives on the line. I just wish I had the ability to help you in the exploration."

She handed the book back to me and I hugged it to my chest. I'd been looking for my mother's face in everyone I'd seen since we arrived in Scotland. Maybe someday I'd find her familiar face. Maybe someday, she'd walk up to me in the streets and tell me she'd been looking for me the whole time.

"Would you mind showing me?" Agnes said, embarrassed to be asking. "I got that display yesterday, and it was truly incredible. Would you be willing to show me what else you can do?"

And not a single one of us minded. Because doing magic was what we truly loved.

THE HORN of our boat did indeed sound sooner than was scheduled. And by the time we all walked outside, we could see why. Just as Agnes had predicted, there was a storm rolling in from the ocean, dark clouds blocking the sun.

"Thank you so much, for everything," Nathaniel said as we hesitated out on her lawn. "You have helped us beyond measure."

"Please, stay in touch," she said. "I get mail at the mainland. I go once a month. I would love to get updates as to what you find." She handed Poppy a piece of paper with an address written on it.

"We will," I promised her. "And you do the same."

"Promise," she said with the nod of her head.

As the first raindrops broke from the sky, we set off back down to the dock. It grew more and more steady as we climbed into the boat, and the captain anxiously pulled away out onto the ocean.

By the time he reached the other dock, we were well and truly soaked.

With squeals and screams and protests against the water, our group ran for their bicycles, and we set out down the dirt roads that were quickly turning to mud.

With the bed and breakfast within sight, I slowed, dropping back to Nathaniel's side.

"Can I talk to you?" I asked, even with water dripping from my hair.

He looked at me through the pounding rain, running through his eyes, dripping off his nose and his lips.

He didn't say anything. But he nodded.

So, we let the rest of the group continue on ahead.

And when I saw the maintenance barn just before the main house, we turned off at that. Ditching our bikes, we ran for the door, which, thankfully, was unlocked.

The barn was huge, really. There was equipment around the edges of it. There were shelves with tools and different parts and things that all looked like they had a job. There were rows of gardening equipment. But at the middle, in the back, there was a huge mound of hay thrown in a pile.

I gathered all of my hair over my right shoulder and squeezed it out, trying to ring the rain from it. Nathaniel shook his head, sending water everywhere.

I noticed he hadn't cut it in some time. And I wondered if that was because I'd told him how much I liked it a little longer.

"I have to admit, I'm starting to think we're never going to find as much as we'd like," I said, turning and looking around the barn. "Maybe we're just going to be on our own in figuring everything out. Maybe we just have to create our own magic."

I felt Nathaniel's eyes on me and turned to look at him and confirmed it. "That would make things harder, for sure. But I think we all have what it takes to do this. All of us. Together."

I nodded, even though I wasn't really thinking about what he was saying. I was looking at his lips. I was watching his hands.

"I feel like we're failing at this," I said, completely off

topic, but they were the thoughts on my mind. "Becoming friends. Learning how to trust each other."

Instantly, the expression on Nathaniel's face grew more serious.

"I told you that you were the love of my life, Nathaniel," I said. My voice was growing rougher by the word, but I wouldn't let it shake. I wouldn't let it waver. "I told you I love you. I told you I didn't want things to be like this between us. But you don't seem to believe me."

There was a war going on behind Nathaniel's eyes. A debate. I could see it clear as day.

Keep things easy and smooth…or say what was really on his mind.

And finally, he made the move I wanted him to.

"It's a little hard to trust when I'm seeing what I'm seeing, from my point of view," he said. And I hated the words, but I loved that he'd said them.

"And what is that?" I asked, prodding him further into what needed to happen.

He took one deep breath, and I could see him preparing himself for what he was wading in to. "I'm seeing the woman I love leaning on another man for emotional support. I'm seeing her asking him instead, to accompany her on secret trips. I'm seeing her smile in a way I was never able to make her smile."

It was true. Everything he was saying, even if I hadn't fully realized it at the time.

"And I'm seeing Borden looking at you with such admiration that I can't help but see the two of you as equals. I'm seeing him, willing to do anything for you, even become a different man from what he once was."

"He's not—"

"But he is," Nathaniel cut me off. "When he first started coming around, you didn't trust him with anything. He joined us out of spite. And now he's spending all day every day committed to this, to you, Margot. He will do anything for you. And how can I even be angry at him for that?"

I felt myself fracturing as I stared at him. Because he was saying nothing that was untrue.

And I hated all the words.

"But how could you not trust me?" I asked, my voice a broken whisper. "I am not the type to lie. I tell the truth, Nathaniel. And I said that I love you, and I always will."

"But I can't tell anymore, Margot," he said in a low breath, "do you also love Borden?"

And with the words, I felt absolute clarity settle into my chest.

I took one step forward as I held Nathaniel's eyes. I took another. And another. Until I was standing right in front of Nathaniel, looking up into his green eyes. Both of my hands rose to the sides of his face, and I cradled him, the way I'd always wanted to, as I looked at him.

"Borden is my friend," I said softly. "And I am very

grateful for everything he has done for me." I held his eyes confidently, and it was killing me that it was only me touching him. "But I am not in love with him. I still want you. Every second of every day. I just don't know how to prove it anymore. Not when we're in this twisted-up place. But I still want *you*, Nathaniel."

There was hunger and anger in his eyes. There was fire and life, and it sparked something exciting within me.

He looked like he could rage and devour.

And it filled me with hungry anticipation.

And I just about exploded into a supernova of satisfaction, when he lowered his face to mine and claimed my lips like he was the god of them. With anxious, frantic desire, his hands came to my hips, his fingertips digging into them, pulling our bodies together.

I couldn't breathe unless it was to suck him in. I took his lips between my teeth, pulling and claiming before coming back to devour him further. My hands wrapped behind his neck, and I crushed my chest to his.

He didn't hesitate a second longer. He hoisted me clean off the ground. With long, strong legs, he walked us a few steps to the huge tractor and the bucket at the front of it. He set my hips back against it and none too gently, he ground his hips into my center.

My head flopped back and he didn't wait half a second before he let his lips trail down to my neck.

My fingers tangled into his hair, keeping him prisoner

within a breath of me. Greedily, I wrapped my legs around his hips so he couldn't escape.

I relished in the feeling as his hands came to my back and slid up into my wet shirt just a little, so his palms were pressed flat to my bare skin.

"I love you, Nathaniel," I breathed out before I could think about what I should say. Needy, I pressed myself closer to him, running a hand up the side of his neck and bringing his lips back to mine.

"This is killing me, Margot," he said as his lips moved with mine, filling me with maddening desire. "We're supposed to be planning our future together. Not avoiding gazes or sleeping in separate rooms."

I couldn't agree more.

"Let's just leave," Nathaniel said as his tongue traced along my ear. "Just me and you. We'll find somewhere new, find a way to reset. Get back to what we know is in our future."

It sounded romantic. It sounded sweet. And it sounded like something that would absolutely work.

But I felt my stomach sink.

Because here we were again.

I pushed him away just a little bit, and his eyes looked hazy and confused at the separation of our mouths.

"This…this doesn't even sound like you, Nathaniel," I said, my brows furrowing. "We can't just run away from our problems." I searched his eyes, begging for him to understand. "We can't just run away. And Mary-Beth and Borden and Poppy and even Olin, they're part of this family now. Do you not see that?"

The focus returned to Nathaniel's eyes, but also, I saw a mournful shadow in them. Of every problem we had.

"I'm willing to do whatever it takes to bring back magic," he said, bracing his hands on the tractor bucket and staring me in the eyes. "But how much am I supposed to sacrifice? Us? Maybe it is selfish, but I will do what it takes to help us survive, Margot."

I shook my head. "This isn't how it's supposed to work. We have to face our problems."

Nathaniel let out a frustrated breath through his nose and stood straight. He turned away, scanning the barn for a moment. "We waited it out, and we survived. The Society Boys have graduated, and now we're never going to have to see them again. Not everything has to be solved with bull horns. Patience and perseverance are virtues."

"The Society Boys were only a mirror to a deeper problem, Nathaniel. We're in college. We have to act like adults. We can't just ignore our problems and wait for them to go away."

"But running right at them with fists swinging is mature?" he roared. And for the first time, I heard Nathaniel yell.

And my chest surged with hope.

If he could fight with me, he could fight when he needed to.

"We do what it takes," I said, really not sure how to do this. "We do whatever it takes for the people we love."

He stared at me for a long moment, searching my eyes. I could tell the gears in his head were turning. I could see words on the tip of his tongue.

But instead of launching them out into the open, he turned, and he walked out of the barn, back into the rain.

I pounded a fist against the bucket, even though it hurt my hand.

But I also felt a smile pull on my face.

Yes, he'd still been infuriating. He still thought avoidance was the best path through problems.

But he'd yelled at me. For the first time, he'd yelled, and for just a few minutes, he'd argued, and he'd fought with me to try and solve our problems.

And I thought maybe, just maybe, we might be able to find our way to a solution.

I waited another minute longer, and then with tousled, wet hair, and swollen lips, I walked back to the main house.

CHAPTER SEVEN

Over the next week, we visited four different towns and stayed at three different hostels. We combed through library after library.

We found one book.

Then another.

And at another library, on the last day before everyone was to fly back to the states, we found three more books.

There were never any leads on people to talk to. We had hoped to find others like Agnes, but all we gained were odd looks and annoyed gruff responses to go back to America.

I didn't tell any of the others, but I was looking for my mother everywhere we went. I had no idea where she'd opened a portal and traveled to. But if she was anywhere in Scotland, I was determined to find her.

But in every face I searched, all I found were strangers.

The night before the flights home, we were all crammed into one room of a hostel thirty minutes away from the airport.

We closed the door behind us, and all of us gathered around to take our first real look at the five books we'd found and, subsequently, stolen.

The first was a book with a fading cover, and the pages within were equally as faded. We could barely make out the words, which, thankfully, were written in English.

Dowsing—one of magical blood can always find water and money when needed. Obtain a pendulum or split hazel stick to practice this simple magic. Hold the stick lightly.

It showed a hand-drawn image with a Y-shaped stick held between a set of hands.

Walk through an area until you feel the twig twitch or the pendulum swing. There, you will surely find water or treasure.

"I've heard of this before," Poppy said. "They're called water witches. They've been for hire in Scotland for years. And sure as day, they *will* find water on a property."

Nathaniel nodded. "I've heard of them, too. Farmers hire them, and more often than not, the spot they indicate will produce a well."

"You're serious?" I asked. "Ordinary people hire a… witch to find water?"

Poppy and Nathaniel both nodded. "I've never heard

of the treasure thing, though," Nathaniel said. "But the water witch part…it makes sense. Because only some people can do it. And if those people are really mages, they just didn't know they really were a witch. I mean, I would bet that even locked mages could do it."

"Not sure how this is useful to us," Mary-Beth said. "Unless we're lost in the desert. Or feel the itch to go on a treasure hunt."

"You never know," I said, raising an eyebrow. "Water is always essential."

I was anxious to give it a try and see if it really worked, but now wasn't the time.

We turned to the next book.

It was filled with old nautical magical tricks. One was a way to calm waves. Another was a trick about tying knots in a rope. When untied, it unleashed wind, which could potentially save a ship in stalled out seas. Another was a way to turn saltwater into fresh. And yet another was a way to call clouds to shelter hot sailors from the sun.

It really was a wealth of magic, though not particularly useful to us, considering we weren't sailing anywhere any time soon.

One book was written in completely unintelligible old English. Nathaniel was sure he could translate it, but it was going to take time.

The fourth book contained instructions for a memory draught. With the right combination of ingredients, it claimed to have the ability to make you recall everything you had ever learned, everything you had ever seen, and everything you had ever experienced. The effects would last seven hours, then the drinker would return to their previous state.

And the very last book contained very, very poorly written instructions on how to trap a soul in an object.

Each of our eyes slid to Olin when we read that. He swallowed once and reached forward to close the book himself.

"You've never talked much about how this person trapped you in that book," Borden said. "Why did they do it?"

Olin continued to stare at the book before him. He was very still and very quiet.

"There were two clans in the area where I lived," he said. "And there were two distinct ways of thinking. At times we aligned, but more often than not, we clashed." He licked his lips then swallowed as if this were a difficult story to tell. His throat bobbed up and down. "My clan wanted to keep working, to connect with the other clans of witches. I thought it would be better if we could collaborate on things. It would make the work go faster. But the other clan…" He shook his head. "They wanted to hunt down Sandris and kill him for what was done."

Olin rubbed his hands together, and I realized then they were laced with scars, almost like bolts of lightning.

They originated on the palms of his hands and raced up the tender underside of his forearms.

"I wanted revenge, too. But with the power he possessed? How could we win? In the end, our clans got into a fight," he continued. "And one moment I was stating my case as things got hotter and hotter. And then the next, it was just darkness. The next thing I remembered was falling to the floor with the lot of you staring down at me."

His eyes rose, and he studied the faces of us all. "I am a man out of my own time. Out of my country. The world is an entirely different place. I've lost all of my family. So, I thank you all for accepting me."

Maybe I was cold-hearted. I should have felt sorry for Olin. What he was saying was terrible. I couldn't imagine having to go through that.

But I couldn't dredge up the level of sympathy he should have gotten.

"Thank you for all you've done to help us," Nathaniel offered kindly. He smiled and then looked around at our group. "We have an early flight tomorrow," he said. "Let's get some sleep."

We were cautious in meeting each other's eyes as we split from the middle of the room to the bunkbeds spread throughout it.

In the time since we kissed and fought in the barn, we hadn't said much. We weren't fixing anything, but in a way, I felt like we were both trying to not make anything worse.

At least he wasn't looking at Borden like he was afraid he was going to lose me to him.

Which told me that I had to do some explaining. I had to do some careful wording, come tomorrow.

But for now, I went to bed, and I slept like the dead.

My eyelids felt like they weighed fourteen million pounds the next day, and it was simply a miracle I made them open. I made myself get dressed extra early, then I tapped Nathaniel on the shoulder, waking him.

Pressing a finger to my lips to tell him to stay quiet, to not wake the others, I turned, and we both walked out of the hostel.

Outside, there were low clouds, casting us in fog. It was a fairly chilly morning considering it was summer. So I wrapped my arms around myself to hold against the cold.

"What's going on?" Nathaniel asked as he rubbed the sleep from his eyes.

"I need to talk to you about a few things," I said. "And my explanations aren't for anyone else."

He gave me a worried look but didn't say anything.

"The reality is, there isn't anything for me to do immediately back home in Harrington," I said. I'd been rehearsing what I wanted to say, over and over in my head, but now that the moment had arrived, it was all gone. I found myself winging it all and praying that I didn't say something stupid. "I am going to try and buy Asteria House, but for now, I don't have enough money. I don't have a job back there. I don't have school. But we still have so much we can investigate here in Europe."

I watched as the pieces started falling into place in Nathaniel's mind as he realized where this was going.

"I will be back," I said as I took one step closer to him. "But I'm not going back until the end of the summer."

The expression in his eyes fell. So, I pushed on. "Just look at how much we found in the past two weeks. In just one country. Imagine what I might find throughout all of Europe, over the course of the next two months."

"By yourself?" Nathaniel asked. "Margot, I know you're a strong woman, and you're capable of taking care of yourself but—"

"Borden is staying with me," I cut him off, needing to rush through this part as quickly as possible. "And I know how that must look to you. But I swear to you, Nathaniel, there is nothing going on between us. This… this is just his legacy, too. It's all of ours. And he now has the time and resources to do this."

I stepped forward, looking up into Nathaniel's eyes.

"I need you to trust me," I said, my voice dropping. I reached forward and grabbed his shirt, bringing our bodies close together. "Nothing is going to change. My feelings are not going to change. It's just time, a few months. It's going to pass anyway. So I need you to wait. And I need you to know I'm not done with us."

I watched as something grew hungry in Nathaniel's eyes. I watched them shift down to my lips.

"I need you to trust me," I said again, feeling desperate for it.

"I trust you," Nathaniel whispered in response.

"I'm not giving up on us," I whispered as our lips drew closer and closer. "In two months, I'm coming home. And we're going to find a way to get through these problems because I'm sick of not being with you. We're going to fix it all, and get on with our lives. Deal?"

Gently, Nathaniel lowered his lips to mine. Softly, he kissed me. Light. Filled with promises.

This kiss wasn't long. It wasn't hard or aggressive. But it filled my entire body, all the way from my toes to my fingertips, to the very ends of my hair.

"Deal," he promised in return.

I found myself smiling as we parted. And the expression on his face was lighter than I'd seen it in months.

We could hear voices inside, and Nathaniel turned to walk back in.

But just then, Borden walked outside, his bag and mine in his hands.

"She just told you, I assume?" he asked.

Nathaniel nodded and stopped in front of Borden. I

watched as he eyed Borden up and down, and I wondered what was going on behind his eyes.

And I was surprised at something I saw there. I saw a confidence I'd never seen in him before. I saw a little bit of a challenge. I saw Nathaniel think of himself as enough for the first time in maybe ever.

"Keep her safe for me, will you?" Nathaniel said. And even though the words were formed as a question, it was said as more of a statement. Almost a challenge. Almost as if Nathaniel were rubbing it in Borden's face that he knew he and I were meant to be together.

And I watched as something changed in Borden's eyes, as well. Almost as if the challenge were accepted. And my stomach tightened.

"I will," Borden said. And I wasn't sure how to feel about his tone.

Nathaniel looked back at me, and for just a moment, it was like I was seeing a new man. I was seeing someone who was going to fight for me. I was seeing someone who was determined to win.

A thrill swept through me, and I tingled from my head to toes.

"Be safe," Nathaniel said.

"I will," I answered him, and I watched as he walked back inside to join the others.

I was saved from having to face Borden's reaction because just then, our bus pulled up. Silently, Borden stepped aboard with our bags, and I followed him inside.

We sat across rows from each other and didn't say a word as the bus drove us to the small airport. When we arrived, Borden greeted the pilot he had chartered. We got settled into our small passenger plane, seated next to six others who would be going on this journey with us.

And I ignored it all as we took off, and made the flight across the water, bound for England.

CHAPTER EIGHT

I RIPPED A BRUSH THROUGH MY HAIR SO HARD, I knew there were strands everywhere. But I whipped through the room, stuffing my things into the bag. And at exactly nine o'clock on the dot, there was a knock on my door.

I opened it, letting Borden in as I walked to the sink and started brushing my teeth furiously.

"Sorry," I said through a mouth of suds. "I overslept."

"The insomnia is getting worse?" Borden asked as he laid four rocks on the nightstand and then set about collecting my things for me.

I spit in the sink and wiped my mouth on the towel. "Yeah. It was about three before I fell asleep."

Over the course of the last three weeks, since everyone left, I had been having trouble sleeping. First, it was an hour that I'd stare up at the ceiling. Then two.

Now it was well and truly the middle of the night before I would finally fall into an exhausted fit of sleep.

There had to be a reason why. I was sure it had something to do with Nathaniel, or maybe the others, considering the timing.

But for now, I was ignoring literally everything in my life except for magic.

Finally packed, I turned and grabbed the rocks from the nightstand. With a tired huff, I sat on the edge of the bed and told myself to calm and collect.

Borden sat beside me and suddenly the curtains pulled across the window, casting us in darkness.

"Spiritus sanguinis mei, et cor meum: ut quod fuerit ferrum, et hoc in clara," I breathed, confident and cool. I took the pin from the nightstand and pricked my finger, collecting among the scars on my fingertips. I touched the blood droplets to each of the rocks.

Swiftly the blood seeped in and started veining out over the surface of the stones. I closed my eyes again and focused on my connection to the rocks. I envisioned them as valuable. I pictured them as having been gold from the very creation of the world. I willed them to be gold. And I reached out to the earth around me. I connected with it, channeling that connection through me to the transforming rock in my hand.

You are gold, I thought.

The hairs on the back of my neck tingled and I felt a

rush go through me. And I knew it was done. I knew the alchemy was set.

Opening my eyes, I handed the gold over to Borden. "Let's go," I said.

He slipped the gold into his shoulder bag and then grabbed my bag to hand to me. I took it, and the two of us walked out of the room.

We'd followed a lead into an old part of England. When we'd heard the name Nightingale, we'd chased it down, searching for William.

I wished Nathaniel could have been with us. He would have loved every second of our search. He would have gasped in wonder at the small village and the library that had a whole section devoted to the witch hunt that had taken place.

But he would have been profoundly disappointed when we'd found nothing more than a record of his name.

We'd spent three weeks here in England, wandering all over the country, following leads. And we had only found two books. We'd found no one to talk to.

So together, Borden and I walked down the road to town. We found a jeweler. We negotiated. We sold the gold. And with a bag full of cash, we headed to the bank.

"You expect me to believe a couple of twenty-something-year-olds have come by this much cash?" the banker asked with obvious mockery. "Don't go anywhere. The police will have some questions for you."

But Borden leaned forward across the desk and pressed his fingers into the man's temples.

It wasn't the first time we'd had to dig through someone's mind to get this done. Sometimes jewelers were too suspicious. Sometimes they'd accused us of robbery. Sometimes they flat out refused. Sometimes the banks had threatened to call in an investigation when we tried to exchange currency. Just like right now.

But I watched as Borden stared into the man's eyes with concentration so fierce, it made goosebumps breakout on my arms. I watched as that man stared at Borden with wide, terrified eyes, frozen in place.

Twenty seconds later, Borden released the man. He blinked four times, still unable to talk. I wondered how it felt, to come out of a mage mind manipulation. I'd never had it happen, because it was impossible to perform on another mage, even a locked one.

But then the man stood. "I'll be right back with your exchange."

"Thank you," Borden said calmly.

We walked out ten minutes later with a massive sum of US currency. We added it to the stash, hidden in a secret compartment of Borden's bag. There was also one in my purse. Another in my suitcase. Another still in a wide-brimmed hat I'd bought, and another in a zipped-up pocket in Borden's trousers.

"We should be wiring all of this back to the States,"

Borden said as we headed toward the train station which would take us to the airport.

I shook my head. "I don't want to raise any questions. That makes me nervous, doing it internationally. I'll take care of it when we get back to the States."

Borden shook his head. "This puts us at such risk. If anyone were to have any kind of clue…"

"Good thing we're mages who are capable of defending ourselves," I said.

We rounded into the train station. And checking the board, we saw ours was just about to leave. We dashed through the small station and barely made it up the ramp and into seats before it pulled out.

We found an empty booth and stashed our bags before settling into seats across from each other.

"I can kind of see how they started happening," I said as I watched the tiny town beginning to disappear behind us. "The witch hunts. If we weren't constantly moving around, I could see someone eventually picking up on what we do. Someone could notice us doing levitation. Or that we always seem to get our way. If we were settled in one town, and we started getting comfortable…"

"You're placing an argument against yourself in establishing a school," Borden said, raising an eyebrow as he met my eyes. "You're talking about gathering us all together. With students who won't be as experienced as us. Wouldn't take much for someone to slip up."

I shook my head. "There's no other choice. We can't just become gypsies. We need a home. We need somewhere safe, within walls to learn. I see what you're saying, and of course it's a possibility. But we're just going to have to be careful."

Borden let out a breath as he looked outside. "I will admit. I thought we'd be finding more. I thought we'd be finding these little nuggets of knowledge left and right. I hadn't taken into account the fact that so few people could read and write back then."

"I know," I admitted. "I never would have guessed this would be the turnout here."

As we rambled down the track, the lights above us flickered and then died. Borden looked up at them. He rubbed his middle finger and thumb together and then flicked it at the ceiling.

Instantly, the blub glowed with light again.

WE ARRIVED in Germany two days later. It was brutal travel that left me craving a bed. I didn't even care that the bed and breakfast we were staying in was overbooked, and Borden and I had to share a room.

I collapsed into one of the beds with a giant sigh and slept like the dead.

"Margot," a soft voice whispered in my ear in what felt like only seconds later.

I felt like death as one eye blinked open.

Borden was there, sitting on the edge of my bed, watching me.

"It's nearly noon," he said. I tried not to read into the soft look in his eyes, the emotions I didn't know how to classify. "We're losing time."

With a groan, I rolled over and wiped the sleep from my eyes. Only, I had forgotten I was still wearing makeup, so I smeared it under my eyes.

"You get showered," Borden said kindly. "I'll figure out our transportation arrangements."

I grunted and made my way to the bathroom.

Thirty minutes later, I felt more alive, and the two of us made our way to the street outside.

This city was huge. It had always been a fairly large hub, but now it was a sprawling city with a population of more than one hundred thousand. Really, most of our interest had been in smaller towns. Outlying areas where suspicion and distrust ran rampant.

But this town had a dark history.

During the years between 1626 and 1631, this town had descended into utter madness, resulting in a witch hunt which brought the deaths of an estimated nine hundred people.

When we learned about this during our time in Europe, my stomach had twisted. *Nine hundred* people lost their lives. That was three times the entire student population at my high school.

But if there had been so many, there had to be some realistic grounding to the reason why.

So Borden and I booked our flights to Germany, and here we were.

The very first place we visited, no matter what, was the local library. In a town this size, there wasn't just one, there were three.

We arrived at the first just after one o'clock. Suddenly I wished I hadn't slept in so long as my stomach gave a ravenous growl as we walked inside.

"We'll get lunch as soon as we're done here," Borden said as he looked around. There were two stories, and as far as I could see, there were three sections on each level. "You want top or bottom?"

I scanned around, feeling overwhelmed. This process took time when we had our entire group. Now that it was just Borden and I, I knew it would take hours.

"Top, I guess."

And so we both set off, our wands held in our gloved hands.

If I had been nervous to travel to Scotland and then to England, I was exceptionally nervous to be here in Germany. At least in the other two countries I had been able to speak the same language, even if some of the accents had been difficult to understand.

But I didn't speak German. I'd heard of their gruff nature, and even if not everyone was like that, so far,

Borden and I hadn't been treated warmly with our very limited interactions.

I wished Nathaniel were here. Even if he claimed his German was terrible, he at least understood some. He could speak it decently enough.

Here, I didn't know any of their language.

So I kept my head down and simply hoped that I didn't draw any attention.

I placed the tip of my wand to the first book and started dragging my pencil eraser along the spines.

Row after row. Room after room.

This library was massive. It took me thirty minutes just to finish the first two rooms. And when I stepped into the third, I found it was the size of the first two combined.

It was difficult to tell what sections I was covering. The titles weren't in English. Even the styles of book covers were different than what I was used to back home.

So I had no idea what section I was in when my wand suddenly turned crystalline and glowed blue.

I smiled and like every other time we had discovered something, a thrill shot through me from my toes to my scalp.

We weren't wasting our time. This wasn't pointless.

I glanced at the inside of the book, but being unable to read German, it meant nothing to me. I glanced over my shoulder to be sure no one was watching, and then slipped the book into my bag.

I finished searching this room, all fifty-two shelves, and then moved on to the last.

Just before I got to the very last shelf, my wand glowed blue once more on the title of a black, worn spine.

It joined the other book once I was sure no one was looking. And then I headed down the stairs to meet with Borden.

I had to wait by the front doors for twenty minutes before he came walking out.

In his hand, he held a tiny book with what looked like only a few pages. He bore a satisfied smile.

"I've got two in my bag," I said in a quiet tone. I took his little book and slipped it in with the others, and with a glance to be sure no one was watching, we slipped outside.

My stomach gave another ravenous protest, so with a chuckle, we headed down the road to a café.

Ordering was a trick, but thankfully one of the employees spoke English and helped us get something. Once we had our food, we sat down at a table on the sidewalk.

"We could really use Nathaniel right now," I said as I dug into something completely unfamiliar. It tasted great though. "I'm dying to know what these books do."

"Let's take a look," Borden said, nodding toward my bag in my lap.

Swallowing my bite, I pulled out the tiny one Borden

found and laid it on the table. I pulled out the one with the black spine. And then I grabbed the last one, which had a soft green binding.

Borden swore. And when I looked up at him, his eyes were wide with shock and fear. He looked left and right as if he were checking to see if anyone was looking.

"What?" I demanded, looking around in concern as well.

"Put the book down," Borden hissed, looking back at me. But his eyes traveled too far up and down me. And they were focused a little off to my left.

With my brows furrowed, I went to set the book down.

I couldn't see my hand…or my arm.

Or any of the rest of me as I looked down at my body.

I swore.

Sharp and snappy, I set the book down on the table, and as soon as I let it go, I became visible again.

"You straight disappeared the second you touched that book," Borden breathed, leaning in closer so no one could overhear us. I looked around, terrified that someone would have seen what just happened, but no one was paying any particular attention to us.

"I don't think it happened when I grabbed it in the library, though," I said in a whisper.

Borden raised an eyebrow. "Were you wearing your gloves?"

"Good point," I said, giving a nod.

Borden took a napkin and carefully opened the cover so he wouldn't touch it with his skin. He did not turn invisible. We both looked at the title, but I couldn't make anything out of it.

"I…I always wanted to be able to be invisible when I was a kid," Borden said with a chuckle. "When the kids talked about which superpower they'd pick, invisibility was always mine."

"Only troublemakers want invisibility," I pointed out.

Borden met my eyes with a smirk. "You didn't know me as a child, Margot. But I also just wanted to be left alone. People can't bother you when you're invisible."

There was something sad about that.

"Well, I'm sure there's something useful we can apply this to, but nothing is coming to mind immediately," I said.

"I'm guessing it will be more useful than you realize," Borden said, and I wondered what he was thinking.

But just then, over Borden's shoulder, I noticed someone eyeing us cautiously. Their eyes were too wide. Too fearful.

And I knew, they'd seen us.

"Borden, we need to go," I said, trying to act calm and cool.

It was like he immediately understood. Suddenly, his shoulders were a little stiffer, and his expression grew serious. He wrapped the invisibility book in the napkin and handed it back to me. I stuffed all three books into my bag and wolfed down three huge bites of my lunch.

Borden set off down the sidewalk, snatching my hand as he passed me. Together, we set off at a quick clip in no direction in particular.

Just as we turned a corner, I looked over my shoulder, back at the man.

He still sat there, ramrod straight, his eyes following us as we retreated.

"Oh, I feel sick," I said when we were half a block away out of eyesight. "That was… As far as I know, we've never been directly seen or caught. Borden, what if—"

"He didn't say anything," Borden said, looking left and right as we crossed a street. He was still holding my hand tightly in his, walking so fast I could barely keep up. "He wasn't trying to follow us. He probably didn't believe what he saw."

I nodded my head, telling myself to believe what he said. But I was still scared.

"We'll lose him, even if he does try following us," Borden continued as he sharply turned us down another street to the left. "We won't go back to that part of town. He'll never find us again."

My heart was hammering, but I told myself to trust Borden. I'd seen what he could do under pressure, and I knew we were safe.

It was others that I worried for when Borden got upset.

Neither of us said anything else for the next thirty minutes as we zigged and zagged and walked down narrow alleys and around corners of huge shopping complexes.

I thought Borden was just aimlessly wandering, until we finally stopped suddenly in front of the university library.

I took three breaths to calm myself down and let go of Borden's hand. Together, we walked in through the massive doors.

To my great surprise and relief, there were signs everywhere, clearly labeling things, in both German and English.

"Can we…stick together in here?" I asked, still shaken from being seen earlier.

"Of course," Borden said, and while my stomach tightened at him stepping closer, something else also sank at the bizarre feeling.

We started in one section and moved through another. Shelf after shelf, we made our way through room after room.

I'd started to get hopeful that Germany was going to be the magic trick, the key to finding magic.

But as we passed shelf after shelf, and found nothing, I started to wonder if I'd been too hopeful.

Until we ran into an end cap display that had the words in German and English.

The dark history of our town: the witch trials that led to the death of nine hundred.

Borden and I looked at each other, hope surging between us like a physical thing. We stepped up to the endcap.

There were half a dozen books on display, as well as a hand drawn map behind glass. I couldn't read what it said, but there were indicators spread throughout the city boundaries. And there was also what looked to be four pages ripped from a journal, two of which had fairly detailed drawings of the trials. One showed a decapitated woman. The other displayed five decapitated figures, burning at the stake.

"As if the decapitation weren't enough," Borden said, a look of disgust on his face. "They had to burn them after."

"Had to be sure they wouldn't find their heads again come nightfall." A heavily accented voice came from behind us.

We both turned to find a woman standing behind us. She was actually quite startling at first. Her hair was dyed black and cut short and blunt. There was a metal rod through her nose. She wore a black backpack and even her fingernails were painted black.

"Did you know that nearly half of the accused and killed were children?" she asked, raising an eyebrow that didn't match her dyed hair. "A large number of them were thirteen or younger."

"That's terrible," I said, and truly, my heart ached for those children, mage or not.

"What else can you tell us about the witch hunt?" Borden asked.

The woman shrugged. "Not much more than what anyone else can tell you. It's just fun to shock the Americans. They're so proud and ashamed at the same time of their little trial. Just over a dozen people isn't much of anything compared to nearly a thousand."

"No, it's not," I said, looking back at the drawings.

"But if it's real dark history, beyond what the books will tell you, it's Hexenhaus you want to visit," she said, eyeing me up and down as if she were evaluating if I could handle it or not.

"Witching House," I said. I didn't know German, but after everything we'd researched, I recognized those words.

The woman nodded. "It's Otto Huber's life's work. It's a bit of a tourist trap, but Otto knows his stuff."

"Where can we find Hexenhaus?" Borden asked, taking out a piece of paper to write down the address.

The woman gave us general directions, and I hoped and prayed it was enough we could find our way.

"Thank you," I said, truly meaning it.

She gave me a little evaluative smirk, one that said I didn't understand what I was in for.

Little did she understand that I was the real deal.

"Come on," Borden said. "Let's wrap things up here.

If we leave soon, I think we can get there before they might be closing."

We practically ran through the rest of the library. Which earned us some dark, annoyed stares. But no one came out and yelled at us, so we kept moving fast.

In the end, we didn't find anything in the university library.

I was hardly disappointed though, because now we had a new lead.

It was pushing five o'clock by the time we walked outside. Borden looked down at his notes again, and we cut down the street to the right.

We turned and cut down streets, according to the directions the woman had given us. We walked under the bridge and then around the corner of the tavern.

And there it was.

CHAPTER NINE

It was an old stone building that looked like it was ready to fall down, only held in place by the black paint that had been slathered over it. It even had a thatched roof on it. And there was a sign hanging over the rickety-looking door, reading *Hexenhaus*.

There was a sign hung on the door that said *öffnen*, which I really hoped translated to open. Nervous and excited at the same time, I knocked on the door twice and then twisted the knob. When I found it was unlocked, I pushed the door open.

It was like walking into a cave of treasure.

There were books lining shelves on every wall. There were maps and drawings spread everywhere—hung on the walls, plastered on tables. There were crystals and cauldrons. The walls were painted a dark blue color, and there were curtains pulled mostly over the windows.

Sconce lighting clung to the walls, and an old chandelier hung from the ceiling with candles still stuck in the holders, covered in a thick layer of dust.

I swear, I could feel magic in the very air.

"Wir sind gerade dabei zu schließen," a booming voice called from behind one of the curtains, and just a moment later, a huge, burly man stepped out. He bore a long beard that touched his chest and unruly hair upon his head. He had broad shoulders and hands that looked like they could rip my head clean from my shoulders without any effort at all.

But despite all that, his eyes were not unkind.

"Sorry for the intrusion," Borden said, undeterred by his gruff appearance. "Do you happen to speak English?"

The man raised an eyebrow just slightly. "A little bit."

I looked over at Borden, and even though we hadn't discussed it, I reached into my pocket, and my hand closed around the change I had gotten at lunch. I held it in my hand and brought it up to my lips. "I just want to know every bit of our history."

It was a truth, and when spoken to a coin by a mage, the recipient could not lie about anything.

"We would like to ask you some questions about your museum," I said, and I stepped forward, handing him the coin. Confused, he took it. "We're happy to pay you to stay open a little longer."

The man looked down at the coin in his hand. I really had no idea how much it was worth. "This would not be enough to encourage me to stay open, in case you were wondering." To my relief, he smiled. "But I am happy to talk, if you are a true believer."

"A true believer?" Borden questioned.

"In why so many were executed in this town," Otto Huber said. "In the real reason why my ancestors were brutalized before their deaths."

A smile pulled in the corners of my mouth as hope surged in my chest.

"Please, share the history with us," Borden encouraged.

A smirk formed on the man's face, and with a deep breath, he launched into the history of the witch hunt in this town. He spoke of three witch families who had lived in this land for centuries. He spoke of their cunning and craftiness. How they could make things grow in seasons when no other could, how they could call the rain. How they could bewitch people.

But one day, a woman was caught coaxing plants from the ground. Another day, a man was caught levitating water straight from the stream to the crops.

And the hunts began.

They killed most of the families within a month. And it spread from there. Soon everyone who did anything out of line was accused of being a witch. And when a surviving necromancer tried to revive his wife after she was beheaded, they started burning the bodies after the beheadings.

"Necromancers were real?" Borden asked, interrupting the story.

"Ja," Otto said, his voice low and grave. "My very ancestors. Few and far between, the necromancers were often feared and misused and misjudged."

"How were the necromancers trained?" I asked, my curiosity deepening by the moment.

This gained me a concerned look from Otto. "Necromancers cannot be trained. They were born. Within certain lines, certain witches were born with the ability to raise the dead. And good for it. Can you imagine if any ordinary witch had the ability to raise the dead?"

No, I could not imagine. What implications would there be? Loved ones reunited? Mistakes corrected?

But maybe I was just too naive to understand the real ramifications.

Otto continued the history, showing us pictures and maps and charts. The witch hunt continued for some time, until finally, they'd killed off such a large portion of the population, all of the real witches went into hiding.

"And then, of course, the Lock of Sandris happened just after that," Otto said, and a chill went straight through my entire body.

Both mine and Borden's eyes flicked up to Otto, and neither of us said anything for a solid eight seconds.

This. This was part of the real history of the mages. But it was not found in any history book.

"The Lock of Sandris," Borden said, his tone measured and controlled. "What can you tell us about that?"

We were making Otto's day, I could tell by the smiles he was giving. Here we were, a rapt audience, who seemed to believe every word he was saying because we absolutely were.

"Two lines of thinking began to emerge in the sixteen hundreds," Otto began his new story. "Those who believed that magic should be used to improve or conquer the world, and those who thought it would eventually bring about the destruction of mankind."

"Euan Sandris," I said, the name slipping over my lips without my meaning for it to.

Instead of being surprised or asking questions why I knew the name, the man just nodded.

"Sandris wanted to eliminate all magic, to put an end to it. And there were those who believed him. Who supported him. But during his travels, Euan Sandris heard of his polar match in England."

This…this was part of the story that we had never heard. I leaned forward in my seat, holding on to every word Otto said.

"They were both powerful witches," Otto continued. "The best of the best. But while Euan wanted to eliminate magic, Bealdor was trying to show the world magic. Government officials and military leaders. He would approach them and tell them. Then show them. He thought he could control the situation. That he could defend himself and his people. But in the end, Bealdor was personally responsible for the launch of half a dozen witch hunts."

Cold gooseflesh broke out over my arms, racing up the back of my neck to cover my scalp.

"Bealdor's determination spurred Sandris to speed up his timeline. He believed it was better for them to lose their magic than to die for it. So, while Bealdor and Sandris' paths had never crossed, Sandris believed he had to stop Bealdor."

This was incredible. This was an entirely different side to our history that I had never heard a word of.

I hung onto Otto's every word.

"Sandris did the rite and locked half of all magic. And while he did not quite accomplish what he set out to do, it was still devastating. And left him weak."

"Weak?" Borden said. "From what we have heard, Sandris obliterated himself in the process of locking magic."

Otto shook his head. "All of his followers who assisted him in the rite were reduced to ashes, but Sandris was powerful. He survived and went into hiding for a time. His body was discovered two months later, with obvious signs of a magical fight. And his body was completely devoid of any traces of magic."

Chills worked their way down my spine.

This was all new information. This was illuminating.

And darker than I'd ever thought.

"Was it Bealdor?" Borden asked. "Did Bealdor hunt Sandris down and kill him?"

Otto shrugged. "It is unknown. But I believe in my heart that is what happened. And I think he killed Bealdor as well, because there is no record of him after that time."

I let out a breath. All of this was…a lot. We knew so little about ourselves, our past, the history of our ancestors.

"Sandris may have saved the witch population from being exposed to hunts," Otto continued. "Surely Bealdor would have gotten all of them killed. But it is difficult to be thankful when because of him, my magical blood is locked away."

My eyes flicked back to him immediately. While it had been there in the back of my mind, the possibility that he really could be the descendant of mages, I hadn't considered that he really, truly might be a modern-day mage.

"I want to try a little experiment," I said as I reached into my bag. I pulled out my gloves and put them on. Otto watched in interest. "See, we're believers, just like you. And we've been working for a long time on creating some kind of test to see who has mage…sorry, witch blood, and who doesn't. Would you like to help us test it?"

Otto's eyes widened and I saw a twinkle of excitement in them. "Of course."

I nodded, and pulled out my pencil. "All you need to do is hold this."

I handed it over to him.

And to my shock, it did *not* glow blue.

Otto was just an ordinary human, who knew real, actual mage history.

"Is that what it's supposed to do?" he asked, looking down at the pencil.

"We're still working out a few of the kinks," I said. I reached for the wand, and he handed it back with a slightly disappointed look on his face, even though he had no idea what it was supposed to do. "Do you mind if we take a look around your shop?"

"Please do," he said, nodding his head.

I gave a nod, and met Borden's eyes. In some ways, it was almost scary how we could communicate without saying a single word. He nodded like he understood exactly and started talking to Otto again, distracting him perfectly, while I carefully started tapping the wand to the first book.

I'd tapped five, when on the sixth, it glowed blue. My eyes widened and my heart leapt into my throat. I moved on.

On the fifteenth book, it glowed again.

On the thirty-first, once more my wand glowed brilliant blue.

On the forty-eighth, Otto finally saw my wand change.

"How did you make it do that?" he asked in wonder.

I squeezed my eyes closed and felt my heart sink.

I knew what we were going to have to do, even if I didn't want to do it.

"Borden, can I speak to you outside for just a moment?" I smiled as I turned, trying to make it seem as if nothing was wrong. And it must have worked. Otto didn't seemed bothered by my request for a private conversation.

"Be right back," Borden said.

We stepped outside and walked ten steps away from the door.

"I've found four books and I've only checked half his shop," I said in a rush. "And who knows what else in there is magical. The maps, the crystals. I have no idea what else could be magical."

Borden looked back at the door. "We can't just leave it all here."

I raised a hand to my hair, letting out a breath in frustration. "I feel awful though. This is his life's work. He's put so much love and effort into this all. And he knows so much truth."

Borden's eyes slid to mine, and I saw he understood how I was feeling. "But he's not a mage."

My stomach sank. Because I knew. "And he'll never be able to do anything with the real stuff he has."

Borden nodded.

Nathaniel had never liked it when I'd altered or stolen memories. And up until now, I hadn't really felt like I was doing anything wrong.

But I felt the guilt eating me alive and I hadn't even done anything yet.

"I'll leave him money," I said. "Enough that he can pay to fix up his shop and find lots more real or fake books. It's…it's not enough, and it doesn't make it right, but…"

"It's something," Borden nodded in agreement.

I nodded, and let out a breath.

"I'd do it myself," Borden said. "But you're still better at it than me."

I nodded, feeling sick about it. But we didn't have much other choice. We had to do what was necessary to further the resurrection of magic. "I'll do it. You start grabbing the books and testing everything else in that shop."

Feeling horrible and heavy, we turned and walked back into the shop.

Otto Huber was organizing things, putting them back into their place from when he took them out to show us.

"I'm really sorry about this," I said, and I didn't give him a chance to react when I walked straight to him and placed my fingertips to the temples of his head.

I felt even worse as I dove into his mind. This was a

kind, good man. This was a man who wanted magic to be real with every fiber of his being. He believed, he knew. But he had no access to magic.

I wanted it for him. I wished that he could have magic, that he could do what he loved so much.

But I couldn't do that for him.

I made him forget that Borden and I had ever come here. I made it so that if he noticed things went missing, he wasn't bothered. I made him not think about the money he was about to receive from us. I told him to do something great with it.

I made it so that he wouldn't ever be bothered by what we were about to do.

But my conscience couldn't just let me take whatever I wanted.

I had to give something back.

So I put it in his mind that, in two years, he would have a burning desire to visit America. He would take a trip to a town just south of Boston, and he would look for a big house on the water, with kind people who lived inside who would want to talk to him.

I gave him hope for answers.

It wasn't a promise that we would tell him everything. That we would show him everything. But it kept the door open for the possibility of someday.

And then when it was all done, I put it into his mind that he needed to go take care of something behind the shop. He would walk out, and then in thirty minutes, he would walk back inside, and he would take the money he would find behind the counter and put it somewhere safe.

I actually felt sick when I released Otto. What we were doing wasn't right. But it was necessary.

"Excuse me," he said. "I have something I need to take care of out back."

I just nodded, and Otto turned and walked out the back door.

I felt a little emotional as I turned and met Borden's eyes while he paused in creating a stack of books that he was placing in a box he'd found somewhere.

He didn't say anything. He just nodded. And continued to take the poor man's real magical books.

I left him a huge sum of money. Enough he wouldn't need to worry about money for a few years probably.

And twenty minutes later, Borden and I walked out with a box full of ten books, two maps, and an array of crystals and clear orbs.

I had no idea what the objects could do.

But I couldn't wait to find out. After my guilt subsided.

CHAPTER TEN

We were hauling around too much baggage by this point. So we found a shipping company. With stomach-twisting anxiety, we packed our precious books into three boxes. We did every bit of magic we could think to protect them. We insured them for a massive sum.

And feeling utterly sick, we shipped them back to the States.

When we got back to our hotel that night, I went to the business center. I paid the ridiculous fee for the call to the US.

I called Mary-Beth's dorm, because Nathaniel didn't have a phone. After four rings, another woman answered, and in two minutes she found Mary-Beth.

"Hello?" she asked, sounding confused and surprised to be getting an international call.

"Mary-Beth!" I said, excited to hear the sound of her voice after a month apart. "It's Margot. It's so good to hear your voice."

"Oh my gosh, Margot!" she said in a breathy laugh, and it made me smile. She sounded genuinely happy to hear from me. I wasn't sure she would. Things had seemed rocky between us. "Hey, Anna, go yell to Nathaniel before he's too far gone."

"Nathaniel was there?" I questioned.

"I'd just gotten in a shipment of books from my grandmother," she explained. "We were going through them."

"Any luck?" I asked.

"No," she said in disappointment. "So much for being connected. So far we haven't gotten a single useful thing from my family."

"But you're pretty much the best for trying," I pointed out.

"Oh, I know," she said, and I could almost see the smile on her ridiculous face.

I heard voices in the background and my heart practically leapt into my throat when I recognized Nathaniel's.

"Is it really you, Margot?" his voice cut through the line.

The smile on my face was ridiculous. "Yeah," I breathed. "It's really me."

There was half a pause, and I imagined the smile on Nathaniel's face. "How's everything going there?"

I twirled the cord of the phone around my finger, feeling giddy with happiness at talking to two of my best friends after such a long separation. "Disappointing in some ways, better than I could ever have hoped for in others."

"Oh?" he asked.

I looked around. The hotel we were staying at was actually pretty opulent, by far the nicest of any of the places we'd stayed so far in Europe. But it was the only thing available in the region. "We found the perfect contact a few days ago here in Germany. No mage blood, but he knew some great new information. And we found an amazing cache of books and other things."

"That's incredible," Nathaniel said.

"Yeah," I breathed out with a smile. Every part of me felt good talking to him—them—again. It suddenly felt like years since they'd all left, not four weeks. "We just shipped you all three boxes full of the books we've found."

"Three *boxes*?" Mary-Beth asked in shock.

"Yeah," I said with a chuckle. "I can hardly believe it either. Most of them are in German though, so I hope you've been working on your skills, Nathaniel."

The sound of his laugh sent a thrill through me. "I have, in fact."

"Good," I said, smiling. "And don't forget your French. That's where we're headed next."

I felt the mood sober a bit as I said the word *we*.

"How is Borden?" Nathaniel asked, and I could tell, he was trying really hard. He said he trusted me. And I was hoping that was how he still felt.

"He's fine," I said. "I think he'd had this idea of finding all of the answers over here. And while we have found some, it's not what he imagined. I think he's more willing to go back to Harrington in a few weeks."

Nathaniel didn't say anything. And I couldn't blame him. For a while, he and Borden were becoming friends. And then things got complicated.

"How is everyone there?" I asked.

"Working like slaves," Mary-Beth piped up. "Nathaniel has us working on magic every hour he's not at the library. And I just watch on the sidelines like a dufus."

"Mary-Beth," I said chidingly.

"You've been getting everyone's genealogy traced," Nathaniel said, correcting her. "We have eight possible lines to trace now because of you."

"Still," Mary-Beth said, "I'm not learning to blow things up with my mind like Poppy and Olin are."

"How are they?" I asked. It was weird in that I'd just started to bond with Poppy, and was kind of starting to learn about Olin when they all left with the others.

"They're good," Nathaniel said. "Poppy is only here

every four days. She's on a rotation with work right now. But we trained her and made her a wand, so she's testing people while she travels."

"That's the other thing we need to talk to you about, boss," Mary-Beth said. And that word hit me in a weird way.

Boss?

"We're thinking it's time to start testing the locals," Nathaniel said. "We have a little extra time to do training before fall semester starts. And with more of us having more experience now, I think we could handle the training now."

My heart jumped in my chest. It was happening. Our plan. It was coming to fruition.

"I think that's a great idea," I said. "I wish I was there to help get it all going. But I'll be back in four weeks to help."

"Hurry up!" Mary-Beth called. And it sounded as if she was walking away. "We all miss you! Nathaniel's a little unbearable with you gone."

I felt myself blush.

Nathaniel chuckled and I could hear him shake his head. "She's a little too intuitive sometimes," he said. "She just headed back upstairs. We have some privacy, so long as no other girls walk by. And so long as I don't get myself expelled for being in the girls' dormitory."

"Such a rebel," I teased him.

I heard him laugh again, and it was nice to hear him

laugh. But the mood sobered, and I felt weight through the phone. "I do miss you though, Margot."

My heart tugged, pulled through the phone, half a world away to Nathaniel. "I miss you, too. I keep thinking about everything, and I'm just ready to find our way through this. I'm tired of this pause."

"Me too," Nathaniel said. "I don't know how we get through it, but I swear we're going to figure it out. I'm sick of not being with you, Margot."

I sighed, thinking of the two of us in his solarium, snuggled up in his bed, his lips whispering along my neck. I thought of his thoughtful gifts of his favorite books, and the flowers he'd picked for me.

"I love you, Nathaniel," I said. The words slipped out automatically, so easy and natural I didn't get a chance to evaluate if it was right to say them. But I didn't regret them.

"I love you too," he answered me, and to my relief, his words were also easily spoken. "Come home to me soon."

"I will," I said.

And as I hung up the phone, I felt a surge of hope for our future. Somehow, we would figure everything out, and we would get back on track.

CHAPTER ELEVEN

I really started to realize the economic differences between Borden and I when we arrived in France. He'd spent quite a bit of time in the country, around various regions of it, even. So he had connections and preferences on where he wanted to stay.

Which, thankfully, lined up with some of our leads with the past witch hunts.

The taxi drove us from the airport to the place we were staying, and my eyes widened as we pulled up and stopped in front of what looked more like a chateau than a hotel to me.

"Surely we could have been more economical with our stay," I said, feeling a little annoyed. I'd left all of the lodging arrangements to Borden, considering I had no idea how to even go about that. But maybe I should have tried a little harder, and we wouldn't be spending so much money.

"But then we never would have gotten to eat Chef Marmont's world-famous escargot," Borden said with a smirk as we stepped out of the taxi and waited for the driver to pull our bags from the trunk.

"I know that's snails," I said, and I could already feel myself turning green. "I'm not eating snails."

Borden grabbed our bags and carried them to the doors, which a footman opened immediately. "It's good to try new things, Margot. You never know what will surprise you with your tastes."

The interior took my breath away. The ceilings soared overhead, and gigantic chandeliers hung from them, making light dance every direction from the crystals hung from them. The floors were a creamy marble. Elaborate woodwork was spread everywhere. And there were great big vases scattered throughout the space filled with white roses. The smell was intoxicating.

Borden went to the counter, and I learned something new about him. He spoke French. Very rocky, from what I could tell of the exchange, it took them a very long time to get things sorted out. But after a few minutes, the man handed Borden two sets of keys.

He turned and returned to me. "You know, if you really wanted to get economical, we wouldn't keep getting separate rooms."

I looked over at him with a surprised glare, but he

wasn't looking at me as we walked down the hall.

"I think by this point you know I'm a gentleman, Margot," he said, and I was surprised how casually he said it. He shrugged. "But we're not much worried about money anymore, are we?"

And I realized then that something had changed. Borden saw me as a financial equal. He was rich, and now he saw me as rich.

I didn't think of myself as such, in any way, shape, or form.

But even as I thought the words, the weight of money was heavy on my physical presence.

There were thousands and thousands of dollars hidden on my person. In my pockets. In my shoes. In my bag. In my bra.

I was currently loaded with money.

"We need to practice," I said as we stopped at the doors side by side. "Meet me out on the lawn after it's dark."

I stepped into my room, and laid on the bed, reflecting on how much my life had changed.

At dark, I went out onto the back lawn of the hotel. It dropped off down a hill, and there were trees everywhere, so I felt fairly secure. A warm summer breeze blew across the grass, and for a moment, I was alone, so I closed my eyes.

I felt all of these connections forming. I felt aware of the life around me. Plants growing, insects crawling around, the birds in the sky.

My entire body tingled with connection.

My affinity was earth. I could feel it, always. I felt its pull and influence with every step I ever took. I felt its call to me and its connection.

But lately I'd been so busy with finding any resources we could obtain, I'd started to lose my connection. I'd hardly done any magic in weeks now. And I missed it.

I extended my hands away from my sides just a bit and turned my palms down to the grass beneath my feet. I kept my eyes closed, and I reached out. I connected with the dirt beneath my feet. I stretched my senses out to the trees, feeling their age and their wisdom. I felt for the sky above me and the flow of the air.

I pushed myself just a little bit. I asked my own body.

And my feet lifted from the ground.

I took in a deep breath, feeling connected, and I felt myself lift even higher into the air.

I felt amazing.

I felt so free. I felt all of my stress and burdens lift from my chest, and for just a few moments, I felt like everything was exactly as it was supposed to be.

I was just me. I was just Margot.

But as I heard the sound of thunder out in the distance, my eyes opened.

I was still suspended in the air. The ground was a good fifteen feet below me.

I should have marveled over the fact that I was levitating myself for the first time ever, but my eyes went right to the horizon.

Where earlier tonight, the sky was blue and clear, I now saw a storm approaching. The first raindrop hit me in the side of the face. And out a few miles away, I saw a bolt of lightning break across the sky.

I turned in the air, even as I began to lower back down to the ground, and there, standing at the top of the hill, I saw Borden, watching me.

I touched down on the grass and walked up the hill to join him.

"What's wrong?" I asked, stopping in front of him.

He shook his head and looked out at the horizon, my proof that he was upset. Because he had called that storm. And that only happened when he was upset. "Nothing," he said. "When did you learn how to do that?"

I shifted to the side of him, watching his storm, even if he wouldn't say what was wrong. "Just now," I answered his question. "I don't know why I'd never thought to use levitation on myself."

"I've tried," he said blandly. "Didn't work."

I shrugged. "I was tapping into my affinity. I was reaching out to all the earth around me, getting centered again."

Borden's look deepened and his eyes narrowed. He

took another step forward and a bolt of lightning streaked across the sky, much closer this time.

He held his hands out in the same way I had. I couldn't see his face, but I imagined he was closing his eyes, tapping into his affinity.

The storm drew closer, just half a mile out in the distance.

Another bolt of lightning struck the ground not far from us.

And Borden lifted right off the ground. Higher and higher he rose, and the storm rolled in to greet him.

Rain started falling on us, growing more intense by the moment.

It was beautiful really, watching Borden be consumed by his affinity, watching him in the air as if he were a part of the storm. He was quiet and calm until he wasn't, and then it unleashed in unexpected ways.

I could feel angst in this storm he'd called. I could feel his complicated emotions and all the pain he'd been feeling.

I wanted to lie to myself and say I didn't know what it was about. But I couldn't.

I shifted beneath one of the trees, which blocked out the rain for the most part. And for five minutes, Borden remained suspended in the air with his back turned to me, being entirely consumed in the storm as wind raged and rain pelted the earth. Lightning streaked across the sky.

And then with one last wind, it all pushed out and the sky grew quiet.

Slowly, Borden lowered back to the ground.

I let out a breath, relieved it was over, but also scared as he turned around and started walking back up the hill.

Borden's eyes were fixed on me, and I saw how determined his shoulders were set, and I knew. Everything we hadn't talked about was going to be exposed, right here and now.

He was dripping wet as he walked beneath the canopy of the tree. I thought he might hesitate, thought he might need a moment to gather his thoughts, but he walked straight to me. He raised both his hands and brought them to either side of my face.

I thought he might kiss me.

But he didn't. He stared into my eyes, and I could feel all the emotions rolling off of him, as real as the storm he'd just created.

"I've kept silent all these months, Margot," he said, his voice low and intimate. "I've told myself that I could endure it and let it go, and everything would be alright." He shook his head. "But it's tearing me apart, and I can't keep it to myself any longer."

I reached up, wrapping my hands around Borden's wrists. I didn't push them away, but I was preparing myself, in case I had to do…I didn't know what.

"It is my fault David Sinclair noticed you, Margot," Borden said. "Because it was me that first said anything. I saw you, on the very first day of your freshman year, and I was astounded." His words were coming out a little faster and harder, and I found my heart racing quicker. "And you were so confident and self-assured, despite the social status everyone wanted to shove down your throat. I expressed interest to James in passing, but David was there, and heard what I'd said."

I'd had no idea. Borden was barely on my radar that first semester. I didn't think he'd even seen me as anything but a target. He'd helped David corner me more than once.

"And David decided he agreed with everything I'd said," Borden confessed, and I watched his expression harden a bit, and I heard thunder in the distance once more. "He claimed you for himself. And I was a coward, and I was selfish, because it made me so angry that he thought he could just order you for himself. But the anger allowed me to tap into my abilities. So I went along with it, hating myself every second. And I knew I would never be worthy of you, Margot. Because despite David putting you, and then Nathaniel through hell, you never backed down, you never bowed to him."

He adjusted his grip on me, shifting just a little closer. And the breath hitched in my throat at his nearness. He was warm, despite the rain he was drenched in. Steam rose from his shoulders, making him seem god-like.

"And it killed me, every day, that I couldn't ever say

anything. I went along with David, torturing Nathaniel, because it grew my self-hatred. I wanted you. And I couldn't have you. So I was determined that I would self-destruct in silence."

My heart was breaking and I felt emotions welling in my eyes.

I didn't know.

I'd had no idea.

I hated all the words he was saying.

I hated that Borden had handled his feelings this way.

I hated that now I knew.

"And I watched you change as you and Nathaniel grew closer and closer," Borden said, his words growing grave. "I saw how happy you were, despite everything we were doing to the two of you. I saw how in love you were. And then, when you and Nathaniel separated, I hoped for half a second. Until I remembered what I had helped in. I knew," Borden shook his head, and I saw how haunted his eyes were. "I knew I would never, ever be worthy of you."

I squeezed his wrists, looking into his eyes. "You're a pretty harsh judge of your own character," I said. My voice came out hoarse. I shook my head as I looked up into his eyes.

"I've been in love with you from the very first moment I saw you, Margot," Borden confessed.

I was breaking. Cracking.

"I didn't know," I said, my voice quiet, little more

than a whisper. "I thought you hated me, or were indifferent and just doing David's bidding. I..." I hesitated, letting my mind fall back to that first semester at Alderidge, which felt like so, so long ago. My eyes met Borden's again. "You and I...we have so much in common. Despite our economic differences, many of our philosophies are the same. The way we handle confrontation, it's the same. We..." My insides were shaking as I spoke. These words weren't easy to admit. Imagining what could have been was tearing me apart. What if Borden had said something that first day? What if he had approached me?

But would I ever have even talked to him, knowing he was part of the Society Boys? Knowing they were his "friends", even if that wasn't the way he truly felt about them?

I was ashamed to say I probably wouldn't have.

So, either way, we never, ever would have known what could have been.

"There might have been something," I said, and the words were so hard to say. "But there were so many circumstances that pointed us a different way. Do you believe in fate, Borden?"

I saw it in his eyes. He was preparing himself to settle, to accept where he knew this was going. And it broke my heart for him. He shook his head. "No, I don't."

And I knew that was going to be his answer. So I nodded. "I believe that what is meant for us will not pass us by. If you and I were meant to be together, we would have found a way."

I could tell I was breaking his heart, but I could also see it had been broken this whole time.

I reached up now, splaying my palm on the side of his face, mirroring what he was doing to me.

"You're one of the most incredible men I know, Borden," I said. I pushed every ounce of sincerity I had into my voice. "You are determined and strong, even if you don't see it in yourself. You walked away from your entire family legacy, for magic. You stood up to the Society. You're forging your path. I can hardly even describe how much I admire you."

I released my hand from him, clinging to his wet shirt.

And I knew. That somewhere, buried deep, there was a possibility. Borden and I would have been good together. Under different circumstances, maybe he and I could have found a way to each other, and it probably could have been great.

But that wasn't what happened.

That wasn't what was meant to be.

"But I am still in love with Nathaniel," I said, releasing him, letting my hands fall to my side. "We have our problems. We still have some things to work through. But I know that he is who I want to share the rest of my life with. He is who breaks my soul out into joy. Somehow we're going to find our way back to each other.

And we're going to marry someday, and we're going to have children together someday, and we're going to run a school for mages together someday." My eyes rose to meet his again. "But that doesn't mean I want to lose you, Borden. You're important. And I always want you as my friend."

He didn't say anything for a long couple of moments. I wondered what was going on in his mind, but I also didn't want to know. This was hard enough.

"You're right," Borden said. "If you hadn't met Nathaniel, I know you and I would have been something great. We would have been happy. But I've spent the last ten months watching you and Nathaniel fall harder and harder. I've seen the way you two look at each other. And I cannot deny it. You and him are something legendary. And even though I know you and I could have been something great, we would never have been that. So how can I fight for you, when I know I can never give you what you have with him?"

Tears slipped from my eyes and my entire body trembled. Because I believed every word he was saying.

Borden reached up and wiped my tears away. Something in his expression softened.

"It's okay, Margot," he said softly. "I love you. And I think I will continue to love you for the rest of my life. But I know how much you love Nathaniel, and how much Nathaniel loves you. So what can I do but stay out of the way of that, and be happy for you?"

"Borden," I said in a breath as more tears made their way free.

He shook his head. "I'm going to be fine, Margot. I always am. I will find my way through this. Someday I'm going to find what you have. And we're still going to be friends, and we're going to be incredibly happy for each other."

I nodded, even though it was hard to imagine. But I wanted that for him so badly.

He dropped his hands from my face, down to my hands, clinging to them. "Please don't let this change things between us. You know the truth now, but I already feel better having it out there. I don't like keeping secrets anymore. Can you please, please still be my friend, Margot?"

And it broke me. Because that was exactly what I wanted.

I threw my arms around him, pulling him into a tight, soul knitting hug. "Of course you are still my friend. You will always be one of my very best friends."

He clung to me tightly, and in it, I could feel all of his pain. But I could also feel relief. We'd been honest with each other. We had no more secrets between us anymore.

And I knew that somehow, despite what normal people might say, we were going to be able to move on now.

CHAPTER TWELVE

The following four weeks passed in a blur.

France proved difficult. Very, very few people were willing to talk to us, and Borden's French wasn't good enough to get us very far. Others were just plain rude to us.

We scanned libraries. Followed the history and the leads. But in the end we found only one book in the entire country.

However, the French were very excited about my golden rocks. When we had little luck in finding resources, Borden and I began shifting our efforts to alchemy and selling the gold.

By the time we hopped on a plane bound for Switzerland, I knew I had enough to buy Asteria House.

Still, that didn't keep me from selling a large amount of gold once we arrived.

To my relief, we found several leads there, and found two books at one library, and then three at another. There wasn't an Agnes or Otto to talk to, but still, we found great information from the museums.

The witch hunts were not purely religiously motivated in Switzerland. Often, they were the result of political differences. And they truly liked to torture their witches. Beheadings and drownings. Beatings and lynching. Some *six thousand* people met their end in Switzerland, accused of being witches.

My stomach turned, the more I learned.

These were our ancestors. Our grandmothers and grandfathers. They were people. And they'd been brutalized for being different. For being able to do things that others could not.

We had to be careful.

I would never, ever forget that.

"This is going to be one of the most important classes we teach at our school," I said to Borden as we looked at a gruesome painting in a museum. "Our history. The staggering numbers. The cruelty of man."

Borden nodded. "Time and peace make us forget," he said. "But we can't afford to. As soon as we do, the world will try to destroy us again."

I nodded in agreement.

We walked out of our last lead in Switzerland with one book.

Somehow, we had truly pulled it off. These four

weeks, Borden and I had spent every single day together, all hours of the day, and somehow, we were okay. Both our feelings had been put out there in the open. We had met them head-on. But somehow, it made everything easier. We'd each said what we needed to. Now, I felt as if our friendship was more solid. And we were okay.

So it was an easy silence we sat in on the airplane that took us back to Scotland. It was easy friendship as we rode the shuttle to the hotel just outside the airport.

And we were just a couple of close friends who were both excited to see my father standing in the lobby.

"I swear you've both come back as full-grown adults," Dad said with a huge smile as I bounded across the room and hugged him to me.

"Well, I guess that's what happens when you're twenty-two," Borden said with a chuckle.

"You've gone off and seen the world, and now I don't feel like I have to worry about you every second," Dad said, squeezing me one last time before looking down at me with a brilliant grin.

"You wouldn't believe how amazing it was," I said. "The cathedrals in France…" I shook my head, recalling them. "You would have loved it."

"I'm sure I would have," he said. "How about we head to my room, and you can tell me all about it? Who needs to sleep before a thirteen-hour flight, anyway?"

Dad looked up at Borden, an obvious invitation.

"I think I'll pass tonight, Professor Bell," Borden said

with an appreciative smile. "I'm already tired. I'll see you both in the morning."

I gave him my own appreciative smile. I knew he wasn't really tired. He'd slept half of the flight from Switzerland to here. But he was giving me some time with my father, when I hadn't seen him in two months.

"Night," I said.

Borden nodded and headed to his own room.

"Tell me all about Germany," Dad said as we walked down the other hall toward his room. "Was it as bloody as history makes it sound?"

And we stayed up for hours as I told him about our travels. He marveled as I showed him book after book, none of which we could read, considering my father was not the linguist of the family. He held onto every single word I said and peppered me with a million questions, most of which, I didn't have an answer to yet.

I wanted to tell him I'd found my mother as well while we had been traveling. In every single country, I had looked for her. I'd searched face after face. I had paid close attention.

But I'd left every country with a disappointed heart.

"What about you?" I asked, pulling back into the present. "How was your study?"

"Just marvelous," he said, smiling wide. "We traced the McGregor line back into the 1200s. I have an entire list for you to look up. But really, it was just fantastic to spend two and a half months in Scotland. It's such a beautiful country."

I happily listened to him go on and on for an hour. And I felt as if my entire body were filled with contentment. This was familiar. This was the way I'd grown up. Talking about history, places, and people. My father had sparked a lifetime of curiosity within me, and I would forever be grateful for it.

THE FLIGHT back to Boston was far more uneventful than our flight out. Each of us settled in with a book, then we each took a nap. It was long, but in the end, it felt like it was over quickly.

My heart started to thunder when we touched down. And not because the flight itself made me nervous.

I was home. And it felt so good to be home.

My nerves were on edge as we made our way through customs. We had to play a few mind tricks to get everyone to ignore the contents of our luggage and carry-on bags. My luggage was insanely heavy when we collected it. Stuffed full of books and hidden money, and the clothes I'd taken with me, it was ready to fall apart from being filled so full. But we made it through with no questions.

We hopped in a taxi and drove the twenty-five minutes back to Harrington.

I was so happy to see our house. The smile on my

face grew bigger as we rolled down the street and stopped in front of our door.

"Would it be okay if I stay the night, Professor Bell?" Borden asked. "I'll need to get a new apartment squared away."

"Of course," Dad said as we climbed out and pulled our luggage from the taxi. I tipped the driver, and he took off. "By now, you need to know you don't have to ask. You all are family."

"Thank you, Arthur," Borden said. "That…that really means a lot."

Because Borden's own father had cut him off. He'd disowned Borden, declared him a shame to the Stewart name, just because he'd walked away from the Society Boys. And then got kicked out of Alderidge.

We lugged our suitcases up the stairs and Dad fiddled with the lock. Finally, the key turned, and we all stepped inside.

"Surprise!"

The lights flashed on, and bodies were springing up and arms were waving and there were smiles pointed in our direction.

I flung a hand out, grabbing one of Dad's and Borden's sleeves as a scream ripped up my throat in shock.

"Sorry!" Mary-Beth said, bounding forward and wrapping me in a tight hug. "Didn't think we'd actually scare you. I thought for sure you saw us all in the window.

"Nope, you well and truly got me," I said, smiling as I hugged her back.

And as my eyes slid over and met Nathaniel's, my insides felt at war.

Peace and excitement. Anticipation and want. Nervousness and elation.

He'd cut his hair again, so it was neat and trim. It looked more blond, considering it was the end of August. There was a golden hue to his skin that told me he'd spent a lot more time outside than normal.

His green eyes met mine, and everything inside of me fluttered.

I wanted to touch him as his eyes studied me. I wanted to match his lips with mine and to feel his tongue tracing its way down my jawline. I wanted his hands greedily grabbing at my hips.

But now wasn't the time. And we had some things to work through first.

So I just nodded at him, trying very hard not to let all these thoughts show in my smile.

From the look he gave me in return, I had to wonder if similar thoughts were going through his head as well.

"Welcome back," a strong Scottish accent said. And I turned to find Poppy, smiling warm and excited in my direction. She bounded over and wrapped me in a hug.

"Thank you, everybody!" I said, beaming with

happiness as I looked around at them. "I think we were expecting to just crash into a bed and sleep like the dead until Monday."

"Never!" Mary-Beth declared. "There are only two more days of freedom left. We party until then!"

She grabbed my hand and pulled me into the kitchen, where I found a full spread of food. I glanced over my shoulder at Borden, giving him a relieved chuckle.

He'd wanted to leave this behind. Family. Friends. He had been ready to spend all our lives searching the dark corners of the world for evidence of mages.

But there in his eyes, I saw that had changed. He was ready. He wanted this, too.

It was a perfect night. Even though I was dead tired and extremely jet-lagged, we had a perfect few hours. We ate food. We laughed. We told stories. But we kept the major things for later. And for one night, I was just gloriously happy to be with the people I cared about.

CHAPTER THIRTEEN

CONSIDERING THAT MY SLEEP SCHEDULE WAS entirely messed up because of all the traveling I'd been doing, and constantly switching time zones, I still woke up at six-thirty on Saturday. And normally Borden was an early riser, but considering it all, he was still dead asleep when I woke up. Even Dad was out like a light.

So I dressed in my favorite white sundress, the one I rarely wore, and I slipped out of the house.

It was peacefully quiet out on the street. Even though the sun was well into the sky, there wasn't anyone out yet. It was as if all of Harrington had decided that this Saturday was for sleeping in. But I smiled peacefully as I walked down the sidewalk and hooked around the fence that divided my neighborhood from the grounds of Alderidge University.

It was strange. Where a few months ago, it was

painful to look at the University because it had once been my home, and then they kicked me out, I felt…different. I felt more grown up. I felt like I had truly moved on and my time there as a student really had come to an end.

I was on to a very different phase of my life.

One thing hadn't changed, though. One thing was looping back around.

I'd waited long enough.

I couldn't hold it back anymore.

I pulled open the gate that had the sign reading: *Warning—Unstable Ground.* I stepped into the abandoned and overgrown garden. I walked past the mossy statues. And then I reached the area Nathaniel cared for, with the blooming rose bushes and the well-tended vegetables.

And then there was the solarium. I didn't see Nathaniel from the outside, but then again, it was early.

A wary smile pulled on my lips as I went to the door and turned the knob.

It was already exceptionally warm inside. With the sun's rays already filling the solarium, it was a good ninety degrees, even with the high windows open.

Everything was exactly the way I'd last seen it. Nathaniel's books were stacked on his makeshift shelf. There was a pile of books on his desk, and I recognized them as some of the ones Borden and I had shipped back. There was a notebook beside an open one, and I realized he'd been trying to translate it.

And there was Nathaniel's bed, with him lying in it. He was half on his stomach, half on his side. His pillow was bunched up under his chin and in one of his arms.

He looked so peaceful sleeping there.

I took a step across the solarium, one and then another, quiet and careful. And then I gently laid on the bed, just looking at Nathaniel.

One of his eyes opened, and he sleepily stared at me.

There were a million things that I wanted to do in that moment, but something in me hesitated.

I was doing this all out of order. We needed to figure things out first, and then we could get to all the good parts.

But everything in me burst with satisfaction when Nathaniel reached a hand forward, hooking it behind my neck, and he pulled me to him.

He wasn't gentle. His grip was commanding and confident. And a wicked smile spread on my lips as I let myself be pulled to him.

My lips found their way to his. They nearly trembled with relief as we kissed. My entire body shook with release and anticipation. Nathaniel's hands came to my hips, and he guided me further over. I was all too happy to hook one of my knees over his body, my hands braced on the mattress on either side of his head.

I sighed into Nathaniel's mouth, which made him smile, and he took my lip between his teeth. I laughed, bringing my hand up to the side of his face, leaning into him as I trailed my kisses from his lips down to his jaw. He tilted his head back in ecstasy as I kissed my way down the side of his throat.

My hands pulled the sheet down, and gloriously, I found that Nathaniel was not wearing a shirt. Greedily, I ran a hand down his chest, appreciating every rise and fall of his toned body.

With a hitch in his breath, Nathaniel grabbed my wrist, and in the same movement, rolled us till I was on my back and he was positioned above me. He ground his hips into mine, sending a blissful sigh rushing from my chest.

Nathaniel dipped his head to my chest, and pressed a kiss between my breasts. Softly, slowly, he made his way higher, coming to the side of my neck. But his hands didn't stay idle. One of them reached back, gripping my ankle, and then slowly slid up over my calf, caressing the back of my knee, and then up the side of my thigh. All the way to my hip.

"Nathaniel," I sighed once his lips came back to mine. My hands rose to lace into his hair and I didn't hesitate in kissing him once more.

I'd missed so many of them in our months of separation. I didn't want to miss any more of them.

Nathaniel and I were cosmic. Our sexual chemistry was galactic in its measure. He brought out animal instincts in me that I hadn't even known existed. And

Nathaniel was always so calm, so in control. Until I got him into positions like this one.

"Zeus's lightning bolt, I've missed you, Margot," Nathaniel said as his mouth again came to my throat. I felt his tongue against my skin, and I nearly lost my mind. I arched back, my chest brushing against his, and I relished in the added contact as our pelvis' pushed against each other. "Next time, I swear I'll go wherever you want me to go. Just don't leave me again."

I sat forward, forcing Nathaniel to sit back on his knees. I crawled right up into his lap, wrapping my legs around his waist.

His eyes looked into mine, and I could have gotten lost for four thousand days.

"I'm not going anywhere," I said, looking down at him. I placed my hand against the side of his neck, relishing that he was here, that he was real. "I'm home now, Nathaniel Nightingale. And we have some problems to fix. But I'm here now. And I'm never letting you go."

Both of his hands splayed across my back, and he tipped his lips to mine.

I kissed Nathaniel like he was mine. Like I could truly claim him as mine for forever and ever. He was marked. He was spoken for.

He was mine.

And I was his. Until the sun burned out, and the entire human race was eradicated from the planet Earth.

Margot and Nathaniel.

"Good gracious balls of feathers, I thought I might find you two like this."

I sat up straight, but there was no hiding the position Mary-Beth found us in. I remained wrapped around Nathaniel's lap, my dress riding up to my hips. Nathaniel was still shirtless, and there was a massive hickey blooming on my neck.

Mary-Beth simply glared and rolled her eyes as she walked in, Poppy right behind her. Poppy turned red from the roots of her head hair, to the tips of her ears and the top of her chest, blushing in embarrassment, finding Nathaniel and me the way we were.

I slid back, easing off of Nathaniel's lap. He grabbed a pillow and held it over his middle as he stood and reached for a shirt.

"I may not officially own this solarium, but over these past three years, I've kind of come to think of it as my own private space," Nathaniel said as he turned his back to us all and pulled a shirt on. "Knocking is helpful."

"Oh, I did," Mary-Beth said. "But I guess you couldn't hear me over all the moaning. Things were getting downright pornographic in here."

I grabbed another pillow and threw it as hard as I could at her. "You're no longer welcome in this space between the hours of eight pm and nine am."

"That mean you two have patched things up and are moving in together?" Mary-Beth asked, raising an eyebrow. "I mean, the solarium has a certain charm, but if you two are going to start playing house, I thought you might pick a real, you know, house?"

"Leave them alone, Mary-Beth."

Cold goosebumps flashed out over my entire body as Borden's voice cut through the solarium from the door. But despite all the hard, all the awkward, his expression was relaxed when he stepped inside and his eyes met mine.

I wanted to cover the hickey on my neck as he walked in and sat next to Mary-Beth and Poppy on the couch. But it was too late. And my decision was final.

Borden and me would never be.

And Nathaniel and I were going to be together.

"I'm not moving in," I clarified, "and we may still have a few things to work out, but—"

"But you're both needy as all get out and had an itch to scratch," Mary-Beth said.

To which Borden grabbed the pillow I'd thrown, and shoved it right into her face.

"You all need to lighten up!" Mary-Beth said with a laugh. "I'm just happy that things are starting to get back to normal around here. Things have been out of balance for too long now."

"Well, I don't think anything will ever truly be normal for us, ever again, for the rest of our lives," I said, raising an eyebrow. "Not when there's magic involved."

And for the next hour, Borden and I brought everyone up to speed. We told them about our travels around Europe. We told them about Otto Huber, about the treasure trove we found in his shop. We told them how unfruitful France had been. We shared all the details, trying not to leave anything out.

"I don't know why I hadn't considered it more," Nathaniel said. He sat next to me on his bed, and even though the others couldn't see it from our positions, he kept trailing a fingertip along the side of my exposed thigh. "During all the time magic had a surge, written language was limited to the rich. Things would have been passed down from word of mouth."

Borden nodded. "There's certainly going to be more out there that we haven't discovered," he said. "But I don't know that we need to invest any more time in searching for more books. We've got our foundation. I think we can build from where we are at."

I nodded. It was nice to finally be on the same page as him. "I'm planning to start making a curriculum this week. We need a schedule, a few basic classes. Borden and I can take on the majority of the teaching since we don't have school anymore, but I'm hoping you two can help as well."

"That's perfect," Nathaniel said. "Considering you already have two new students who are ready and anxious to start learning."

I looked over at Nathaniel with wide, shocked eyes.

"We started testing people in town," Mary-Beth said.

"There aren't many students around this time of year, so we started with all the real grownups."

"She's underselling it," Poppy corrected. "We've tested nearly the whole of Harrington."

"I don't think there are many we could have missed," Nathaniel said with a nod. "We've found two others. And we'll resume testing as soon as school starts on Monday."

"That's amazing," I said in a breath. "Two more. And who knows how many more there will be when all the students come flooding back."

I looked over at Nathaniel, and a thrill flashed through me at the look in his eyes. "Looks like you better find a place for your school to start operating."

A smile grew on my lips, and I knew then that I was ready.

The next seven days were utterly surreal.

I met with the real estate agent. We put together my offer to the Asteria family. And within twelve hours, we got a response.

They accepted my offer.

It was a whirlwind of bank visits and title company signings.

And on Friday evening, I walked down the road and met the agent outside.

He set a ring of keys in my hand and told me congratulations.

It was pointless, the keys. Because the house was so broken anyone could wander in any time.

But still, tears pooled in my eyes as I looked at the decaying house.

It was mine.

I'd done this. I'd made enough money and I'd purchased it.

The windows were broken and parts of the roof were missing. It had been broken into, and there were whole sections of the floor that had rotted out.

It wasn't a home yet, but it would be.

"You're really quite amazing, Margot Bell."

I startled at the voice behind me. I turned to find Nathaniel walking down the road, his eyes fixed on me.

He came to stand beside me, and we both looked at the house.

"You set your mind to it, and you made it happen," he said, taking it all in.

"I never would have imagined it when you brought me here last fall," I said, shaking my head. "Can you believe that was a year ago?"

A year ago almost exactly. Very nearly to the day.

"Yes and no," he said. "In a way, it feels like that was just last week, but at the same time, it feels like a whole lifetime ago. So much has changed since then."

I nodded in agreement, because I felt the exact same way.

"Want to help me finalize my plans?" I asked, smiling as I raised an eyebrow at him.

"I'll follow you anywhere," he said.

And even though we still hadn't figured anything out yet, I reached a hand out and took Nathaniel's, lacing our fingers together.

We walked through the house, and I went off on the cabinet design I'd seen in a magazine and fell in love with. I talked about how I wanted a stained-glass window in the main living room, and how I wanted the floors to be restored to their original color.

We walked through the upstairs, and together, we counted off how many students we could house here. In the end, we determined we could handle eighteen students if they shared rooms. And that was leaving four bedrooms to ourselves and the others.

We wandered back downstairs, and then we stepped into the master bedroom.

It was positioned on the north end of the house. There were windows all around the room, giving an impressive view. Amazingly, most of them were still intact. There was a large bathroom attached to it, with the most beautiful clawfoot tub I'd ever seen.

"I cannot wait until there is running water again so I can climb into this and just relax," I said, running my hand along the edge of it. "With hot water and that view…"

Nathaniel smiled and shook his head. "You know, I've

refused to take a bath since I was about eleven years old. Only showers. Even if it caused me troubles."

My brows furrowed together in question.

"I lived in this foster home," he said, sitting on the edge of the empty tub. "The one with all the cats?" I remembered him telling me about it, how it smelled awful. "They only had a bathtub in the house. They never cleaned anything. That included the tub. So it was always full of cat hair and human hair and had a perpetual brown ring around it. It was disgusting. So after I moved out of there, I refused to ever get in a tub again."

I hated hearing stories of Nathaniel's upbringing. But at the same time, I loved hearing the stories. Because they helped me understand him better.

"Well, maybe there is a way I can make you like bathtubs again, someday in the future," I said, walking my fingers along the edge of the tub until they crawled up Nathaniel's leg.

His eyes burned with curious intensity as they met mine, and I relished in the smile that pulled in the corner of his mouth. "Perhaps someday I could be convinced."

I smiled, blushing a little, even though I meant every word.

I reached for his hand and continued walking through the house with him. We walked up the spiral staircase that always left me questioning my survival chances. We stepped out into the office at the top of the tower.

"The headmasters have to have their impressive office, right?" I asked, looking out over the spectacular view of the Atlantic Ocean.

"Headmasters?" he asked.

I leaned into him. "If there was anyone in the world more suited to be a headmaster than you, I wouldn't believe it," I said. I breathed in deeply, relishing that we were here again, together.

"You have so much faith in me," he said quietly.

"I know," I said. "And it's well deserved."

He let out a noise that was neither negative or affirmative.

"We need a new name," I said, moving on. "Asteria House does sound beautiful, but considering it no longer belongs to that family, I think we need to change it."

"You don't want to call it the Bell House?" he asked.

I just laughed and hugged myself tighter to him. "Doesn't have quite the same ring, does it? And I think I want it to be some kind of school title. I might own the house, but it has never been just about me."

Nathaniel didn't have an answer just then, and neither did I. So for now, he leaned his head on mine, and we stood like that for a long, long time, staring out over the ocean, imagining the future.

CHAPTER FOURTEEN

"Out of the last ten clients who have hired you, how many of them did you overcharge?" Mary-Beth asked, staring the man straight in the eyes.

"Nine," he answered. And we knew it was the honest truth, because he held a coin of compulsion in his hand.

Mary-Beth's lips went into a thin line and she nodded. "Thank you for coming in. You can go now, and maybe apologize to all those people you ripped off."

The man's brows furrowed and there was a scowl on his face. But he stood and walked for the front door, being careful not to fall down into the hole just in front of it.

"Next!" Mary-Beth yelled, so loudly, I winced.

Another man walked in, one of the last two in a long line of contractors.

I'd put out an ad. And to my surprise, every

contractor within fifty miles had shown up to look through the house and go through my proposal of what I needed done.

Now, Mary-Beth and I were interviewing all of them.

We needed honesty to know who wasn't going to screw me over. And thankfully we had a fool proof way of getting it.

"Brent Flagstone," Mary-Beth read off of his resume and his proposal as he sat down on the old couch across from us. Mary-Beth and I sat behind a desk we'd lugged in from one of the rooms and sat on two rickety chairs that were likely to give out at any moment. "You normally work in Boston?"

While she asked the questions, I took a penny from the tabletop and clutched it in my fist.

"I'm not even sad about being expelled anymore," I confessed to it, bringing my fist to my lips. When it was done, I stood and walked toward Brent, extending it to him. He took it with confusion, but didn't ask any questions.

"Yes," he answered. "This job would be a bit of a drive, but I've always admired Asteria House and thought it was a shame the family let it go. This would be an incredible opportunity to restore it to what it once was."

I nodded, liking that he had an appreciation for the house, the same as I had.

"And what did you think of the proposal?" I asked, looking down at the packet I had in front of me. In it, I had outlined everything I was looking for, in great detail. "Do you think it will all be feasible?"

Brent nodded. "All of the interior fixes will be no problem. The exterior will be a little more of a challenge. And I don't think there's any way we can fix up that pool for the price you're looking for."

I appreciated that he was being honest about that. "Double?" I asked.

"More like triple," he said. "It's largely going to be started over from scratch."

I sighed. I didn't love that idea, but I did really want the pool.

"How confident are you that you can stick to this budget you've proposed?" Mary-Beth asked, pointing at the total at the bottom of one of his pages.

"Exceptionally," he said. "So long as it isn't including the pool."

Mary-Beth looked at me. His bid was the second best, but the other guy apparently had a reputation for underbidding and then getting homeowners to pay top dollar in final stretches of panic.

"Do you plan on ripping me off while you're working for me?" I asked.

His brows furrowed at the honest question. "No, ma'am. I put a lot of value into my reputation."

"And are you ever going to have any issue working for a young, single woman?" I asked, leaning forward, because this was something I was greatly worried about.

Just from looking into his eyes, I trusted Brent.

"My mother was seventeen when she had me," he said, and I knew it was the truth. "She raised me on her own, and did an incredible job doing it. I think you buying this house on your own is pretty impressive. So no, it isn't going to be a problem for me."

I looked at Mary-Beth, and silently, we had a conversation.

Twenty seconds later, we both looked back at Brent. "If you can start this week, you're hired."

A big grin spread on his face. "Yes, ma'am. Looking forward to it, and I appreciate the opportunity. I'll be here the day after tomorrow."

I smiled as I stood and shook his hand. "I can't wait to see what you can do."

CHAPTER FIFTEEN

"What are you working on?"

Despite all the noise going on around me, I still startled when a voice came up from behind me. I whipped around at the desk to find Olin standing at the top of the stairs.

He looked so normal now. His hair had been cut in a modern style and he wore clothes befitting our time. Only his eyes held any kind of hint that something was different about him, that he was a man out of time, over three hundred years away from everything he'd known.

"I'm working on a curriculum for the new students," I said as my heart slowly returned to a normal rhythm. "It's proving a bit challenging to figure out how to fit Poppy into all of this. With her schedule, she's missing half of everything."

"It will be worth it though, in the end," Olin said as

he walked further into the office and looked down at my desk and the schedule I was working on. "What she'll bring. I believe she's going to find other mages at some point, and the more students we get, the more successful we will be in resurrecting our species."

I looked back down at the schedule and nodded.

Borden and I would be taking most of the load in teaching. Since we didn't have school, that left our days entirely free. Nathaniel would teach two evening classes per week, and Mary-Beth would help in whatever ways she could as many days as she wanted.

It was too bad she wasn't a history buff. She didn't need to be able to do actual magic to teach the students about our history.

"Telekinesis," Olin said, reading off of the page. "Healing. Transfiguration. Applicable daily magic. What's that one?"

I leaned back in my seat, slightly annoyed that he was interrupting me. "Just a combination of daily uses of magic. We've found plenty of books that had random, seemingly inapplicable magic. But we've picked out tidbits here and there that we can combine into a useful course."

"I'll be excited to take that one myself," Olin said with a smile that looked a little fake to me. He looked back down at the page. "History is the number one requirement though. Why's that?"

I looked up at him and raised an eyebrow. "Really?"

His brows furrowed in confusion.

"With everything you lived through, you don't think it's important for the students to learn about their history? We don't need to re-collect all the mages only to have history repeat itself and have us be wiped out again."

Olin sat on the edge of my desk, and that greatly annoyed me. "I believe we should not have to live in fear. It's a new age. There are new laws that protect all, are there not?"

I continued to glare at him.

"Mages have incredible abilities to protect themselves. All they have to do is learn. So why create an attitude of fear? That's not much of a way to live."

"The idea sounds nice and certainly sounds modern," I said, mulling over everything he'd just said. "But I do not believe the world has progressed as much as you might think."

He looked out at the ocean, and I wondered what was going through his head. I didn't know hardly anything about him yet. He shared stories from the past, but only so many. He had advice every once in a while, but for some reason, everything he said felt shallow to me.

I told myself that I just hadn't had enough time yet. I didn't have those two months with him that the others did.

In time, surely he wouldn't rub me the wrong way so much.

"How are things going up here?"

I turned to find Borden walking up the stairs.

And instantly, I felt a rush of relief to not be alone with Olin any longer.

"I'm just here being a distraction," Olin said, displaying a smile. He stood, finally getting off my desk. "I will leave you to it."

I didn't say anything as he stepped to the stairs, moved around Borden, and walked down and out of view.

My eyes slid over to see Borden doing the same thing.

"There's something about him," Borden said.

"Exactly," I said. "He hasn't done anything to make me not trust him, but I don't. And I can't put my finger on why."

"I agree," Borden said. "I could have him followed. I know a man."

My eyes slid over to Borden then and I barely resisted the eye roll. "Really? That may be overreacting just a little, don't you think?"

"It's not very often that I overreact," Borden said as he took a seat in the one pushed against the wall. Like everything else in this house, it was falling apart and really probably wasn't safe to sit on. Brent had tried to tell me I couldn't even come in the house while he and his crew were working, that it wasn't safe. But I'd insisted.

Now that it was mine, I wanted to be here. I wanted to experience it. I wanted to start my life here.

So here I was, every day, in this tower of an office.

"I've got a preliminary teaching schedule," I said. "Since the house won't be finished for six months, we're going to have to get creative with our locations. But I think we can come up with something. Especially since we only have two students right now. Well, and Poppy when she's here."

"We can use my apartment," Borden said. "It's not particularly big, but there's a spare bedroom. And I know Nathaniel is always open to letting us use the solarium."

I nodded. "That's the plan. He's going to teach the telekinesis class there."

"We're assigning subjects then?" Borden asked.

I nodded. "Telekinesis seemed fitting for Nathaniel, considering that's how this started, with him finding that book. I think you and I should co-teach history, considering everything we learned and saw in Europe. What do you think about that?"

Borden nodded. "Sounds good to me."

"That's two classes covered," I said, tapping my pencil against the paper in front of me. "I also think we can teach applicable daily magic together."

"That's a mouthful," he said with a smile.

I chuckled. "I know. I never said I was good at naming courses. We can figure out something better later. That leaves healing and self-defense."

I had my thought on who would take what, but this

wasn't just about me. Borden and I were partners. I trusted him in this too.

"My healing abilities are still somewhat shit," Borden said, a small smile curling on his mouth. "So I think you know what my vote is."

I smiled and wrote it down on the page. "I'll take healing and you get self-defense."

Borden nodded in agreement.

"That sets our first semester," I said. I leaned back in my seat and propped my feet up on the desk, taking my schedule into my lap. "I'm thinking a three-semester schedule. Classes will start in the fall, same as at Alderidge. Each semester will be twelve weeks long. And we'll always have a summer break."

"You're kind of a natural at this, aren't you?" Borden asked.

I smiled, feeling myself blush slightly. "I guess that's what happens when you are raised by professors."

And instantly, I felt the mood sober. My stomach twisted and my throat got dry.

"I'm really sorry we didn't find her, Margot," Borden said softly.

I nodded. "It's okay. I knew the chances were exceptionally slim. If my mother is out there in the world, stuck for four years, it wouldn't be in a place like Europe. She could be in the Congo or the Amazon, or just about anywhere."

"We could always try the portal magic," Borden

pointed out with caution. "If there's any chance of finding her, it might be with the same thing that made her disappear."

My throat grew tighter and I shook my head. "No," I said, my voice hoarse. "I would never put anyone else at risk."

He didn't say anything, but just his presence was support enough. I knew he was there for me.

"It's kind of insane to think we're really doing this," Borden said, moving on. "Starting a school. Teaching others. We've just found a whole slew of new magic that we can't even try yet until Nathaniel finishes translating. We barely know what the hell we're doing ourselves. Now we're supposed to be in charge of others?"

I nodded, cracking a little smile. "It's true though. It's insane to think that I only learned about magic a year ago. And now I'm here." I looked around, indicating this house, but everything else, too. "But it feels right, don't you think?"

Borden shook his head and shrugged. "I suppose. It's different for you than me. You always planned to teach. I was supposed to be traveling back and forth from China, securing huge international finance deals for my father's company. And now we haven't spoken in five months, and my name has officially been removed from the company."

The words of *I'm so sorry* were on the tip of my tongue. But I'd said them dozens of times already.

"Maybe you were supposed to end up here all along, too. You just needed a harder push in the right direction."

Borden's eyes slid over to meet mine, and a mischievous smile cracked on his lips. "You and your belief in fate."

Just then, Nathaniel walked up the stairs, and I turned to greet him with a smile. "How do you feel about teaching telekinesis in your solarium?"

Nathaniel rested a hand on the back of my chair. "That sounds great." And I could tell he genuinely meant it. "This the curriculum?"

I nodded.

"She's already got it all mapped out," Borden said, and I didn't miss the admiration in his voice.

"Though I'm open to input from both of you," I said, and I couldn't help but relish in the peace I felt, being here, with the two of them, doing what we loved.

"I'm happy to help however I can," Nathaniel said, and I marveled at the constant sincerity in his voice. "And after next spring, I'm all yours."

That brought heaviness back into the room. And my stomach yanked in an impossible direction when Borden stood.

"I've got to get back to work," he said. "Still not looking to become a financial dependent. The markets await."

I wanted to say something comforting, but I was at a loss for words.

Borden had confessed he was in love with me, but he knew I didn't feel the same way, but that was quite possibly because of timing.

How was that supposed to make him feel? Being alone in his feelings, yet knowing things could have been different if the other man in this room had not come into the picture?

"Thanks," was all I said instead, because I didn't know what else to say.

He just gave a nod and headed down the stairs.

I looked up at Nathaniel, and we both just looked at each other for five very long seconds.

"Want to go down to the beach?" I asked, because the air here had grown too thick.

"Sure," he answered.

We made our way down the spiral staircase. There was a full crew of ten men going to work on the house. They'd been here for a week, and already the space was transforming. The floors no longer had holes. All of the broken windows had been torn out, and they were shoring up every rotted-out piece of wood in the house.

Nathaniel and I cut through the living room to the master bedroom. We stepped out onto the deck that did still sag and worked our way down the stairs.

The grasses were exceptionally tall right now, being the end of summer and the beginning of fall. Someday, I'd have to put some thought into landscaping. But for now, we made our way down the bank and out onto the sand.

It was a little windy, but the air was warm, and the sun was shining. Which left me hopeful for Borden. At least there wasn't a storm brewing. Though I was sure the wind was due to him.

Nathaniel and I made our way halfway down the beach, and I plopped right down in the sand.

And even though I knew he hated the sand, Nathaniel sat down beside me.

It was kind of beautiful. Us, together, sitting out in front of my house, in the sunshine. It was one of those moments I wished could be put on pause, wordless, for a few days.

"I think we should hire a translator," Nathaniel said, because we can't always get our wishes.

I looked over at him, my brows slightly furrowed. He looked at me in return, and I saw vulnerability in his own eyes.

"My German is progressing, but we can't afford for me to make mistakes," he said. "We need those books, and we need them as soon as possible. I'll finish translating the French one by tonight. But the others, especially the Swiss ones, we need someone else, Margot."

I could tell Nathaniel hated the idea, but he had the maturity to know what needed to be done. He wanted to be the one to discover every precious word, and as a linguist, he had the skills. But it was going to take time.

"Okay," I said. Because it had never been an issue for me. "We'll find translators."

"It will be expensive," he said. And this had always been a sore spot for Nathaniel. He'd never had any money, his whole life.

I never had either, until I learned alchemy.

Was that cheating?

Not really, because I still had to have the skills and abilities to execute it.

"It doesn't matter," I said, shaking my head. "We need those books. Every bit of gold I sell, it's all to finance this. All of it. The house. The school. Any supplies we're going to need. Travel, if need be. Translation of magical books certainly falls into that category."

Nathaniel looked away, out over the ocean, and nodded.

"What do you think about Olin?" I asked, recalling the few moments I had with him earlier.

Nathaniel shrugged. "I don't know. He's kind of difficult to get to know. He's so overwhelmed by the time change, and I think he's still grieving the loss of everyone he knows. He's trying to hide it, but it has to get to him."

I wasn't sure I agreed. I didn't get that same impression.

"He's a very curious man though," Nathaniel said. "He's always asking questions. He wants to understand how everything works in our modern world. He's always interested in the translations. He's been asking me endlessly about the history of what happened in other countries during his lifetime."

"That surprises me a little bit," I said, finally voicing how I felt. "When he saw that history was going to be my number one requirement, he questioned me. I had to explain it to him, and then he gave me this little bit on not living in fear."

Nathaniel nodded. "He's talked about that before. He thinks things could be different now because laws would protect us."

"What's your opinion on that?" I asked. The very thought made me squirm and want to break out into hives.

He shook his head. "I think our founding fathers had a great vision for our country. But I don't think that vision will always be executed in a just way. The system is only set up to handle things within the people's definition of normal."

I nodded. "Exactly. We think we're progressive and modern, but when it comes down to it, when the masses feel threatened, everything can change."

"I'm with you, Margot," Nathaniel said, and he leaned toward me, his shoulder brushing mine. "I will talk to Olin. Explain how it is. He will understand eventually."

I nodded, even though I wasn't so sure.

CHAPTER SIXTEEN

A KNOCK AT THE FRONT DOOR OF MY FATHER'S house pulled me downstairs at one in the afternoon on a Thursday. I opened it to find Mary-Beth standing there, a look of excitement on her face.

"Come on," she said with glee. "You've got to see this."

"What?" I asked, even as she pulled me out the door without hesitation.

"You have to hurry, class will be out in fifteen minutes."

She hardly even gave me a chance to talk, because she pulled me into a run, and together, we sprinted across the campus grounds.

I hadn't stepped foot back in the doors since I finished cleaning my mother's secret office out five months ago. It felt surreal as I walked through the halls. I had grown up within this school, but now I felt like a stranger.

And I was okay with it.

I knew my purpose in life now.

"Come on," Mary-Beth said as she pulled me down the linguistics hall. We walked halfway down and finally, we stopped in front of one of the French room's doors.

"Look," Mary-Beth said, pointing through the small window that allowed us to peek into the class.

I looked, and immediately, I knew what she was pointing at.

There were two young women sitting at desks that were side by side. From their looks, they were obviously twins. And both of them held pencils that were glowing brilliant, crystalline blue.

"Nathaniel and I have been switching out the entire school's supply of pencils since school started three weeks ago. So far there's been nothing. But I was headed to the library earlier when I walked by and looked into the window, and there they were."

"That's amazing," I said, shaking my head. "How did you invite the other two in?"

"Nathaniel just struck up a conversation with them," Mary-Beth said as we continued to watch the girls through the window. "He said he tested them first. I'm bound and determined to be the only special informed locked mage."

She was making it a joke, but I knew how difficult this still was for her.

"And he just kind of kept talking to them to feel them out. And eventually, we all just told them."

"Think you want to be the spy for these two?" I asked.

"I'm pretty certain I'm up to the challenge," Mary-Beth said as she dramatically laced her fingers together, extended them forward, and cracked her knuckles.

I could only laugh.

My nerves were high the following Monday. We were all meeting at the solarium in twenty minutes for our first official class.

This wasn't the way I had planned to run the school. We were starting three weeks late. We had no official space. This wasn't any kind of split, dedicated class.

But until the House was finished, we would adapt.

I walked down the garden path and then to the door of the solarium. I knocked once before I walked in.

Nathaniel was already inside, as was Borden. The two of them were moving Nathaniel's desk against the stone wall to give themselves some more space to practice in.

"Is everyone else as nervous as I am?" I asked as I watched them.

"Nothing will ever be as nerve-wracking as when I told you, Margot," Nathaniel said as he wiped his hands on his trousers, even though there was nothing on them. "But instructing four new students at once is certainly a new level."

"We have three teachers," Borden pointed out. "I think we can manage."

"You have a point there," Nathaniel said, raising his brows slightly. "I am grateful that I have you all to help get my first class started."

I wouldn't confess it out loud, not right now with Borden here. But it kind of turned me on, Nathaniel talking about his class.

And suddenly, an entire fantasy sprung to life in my mind. Of me walking into his office. Of him taking charge.

I blinked, hoping I wasn't flushing.

That was something to explore later.

There was a rustle outside, and I turned to see four people walking along the side of the solarium to the door, Mary-Beth leading the pack.

She didn't hesitate when she got to the door. She simply swung it open, and invited everyone inside.

As I had once done, they all looked around at the solarium with wonder and surprise. Its existence was long forgotten, and seeing it converted into a living space was nothing short of magical.

"I always thought this place was haunted," one of the men said. "Or massively infested."

"This place is incredible," one of the twins said. "I

mean, I don't think I could live here, but it's kind of adorable."

"Welcome to my home," Nathaniel said with a chuckle. "I guess introductions are in order."

"As if any of us don't know the four of you," one of the twins said. She wore a mischievous smile, one that said she was entertained. "You and Margot are pretty infamous at this point as a power couple who is always on and off again."

My eyes slid over to Nathaniel and I felt myself blush, because it was kind of true.

"And then the entire school knows about Margot and Borden's escapade in knocking the Society Boys down a few pegs on the pride board," her twin continued. It was creepy, they even sounded the exact same. "And then Mary-Beth is always putting everyone in their place."

Mary-Beth made a dramatic curtsey movement, taking a bow.

"I'm not sure how I'm supposed to feel about our teachers being younger than myself," one of the men said. "I mean, you can't be a day over eighteen."

I was annoyed when he indicated me. "I'm almost twenty, thank you very much."

He just chuckled and shook his head. But it was playful, and I could tell he wasn't trying to truly offend.

"Look, I know everything about this situation is strange," I said. "We don't look like teachers, and really, we're still learning a lot ourselves. But we're all in this together. We're on the same team, and if you're willing to become a part of this family, we can teach you incredible things."

They looked around at us, and I could see the evaluation in their eyes.

"This sounds a lot more fun than getting that useless French studies degree my mother is pushing me toward," one of the twins said. She stepped forward, extending her hand. "I'm Marie Daniels."

"Julie," her twin said, also shaking my hand.

"Someone tells me I have magic in my blood," the tall one with black hair said as he stepped forward, offering me his hand. "I'm in. Dorian Engel."

I smiled as I shook each of their hands.

"This all sounds like madness to me," the last one said. "But who wants to live a boring life? John Hunsaker."

I shook his hand, smiling as my chest filled with anticipation. Each of them moved on to shake Borden's hand as well. And I felt a little bad for them. Because Borden's resting face was not inviting. It was ever suspicious and doubtful. Because that's how he naturally was.

"We're really happy to have you all here," Nathaniel said, and from the look on his face, I could tell he meant it. "We know you all have lives outside of this, so our class schedule is going to be flexible. But we'd like to start our first lesson with a little telekinesis."

A smile grew on my face at the look on each of their faces.

I'd almost forgotten how exciting this part was. Sharing this real magic with someone new. Watching their excitement and wonder when they actually performed it.

And it was one of the best experiences in the world as we spent the next hour and a half, teaching all four of them how to make things float with only the power of their minds and the magic of their blood.

"That's very good, John," I said as I leaned over his shoulder and observed the steam rising from his mug.

We were learning fire starting and using it in daily life. We jokingly called this the DAM class, because Daily Applicable Magic, was a mouthful. No surprise who gave it the nickname—Mary-Beth.

We'd been working for two weeks now with our four students. While some days we met at Borden's apartment, usually we met in the solarium. It was closest to school and, therefore, the easiest, even though neither John nor Dorian were students at Alderidge.

"How is this so easy for all of you?" Julie complained, still working on lighting the wadded-up paper in the fireplace.

"It likely has something to do with your affinity," I pointed out. "Maybe we'll come to learn yours is water."

"Sometimes it helps to think angry thoughts," Borden said, to which I glared at him. He just smirked and snapped his fingers. Julie's paper instantly lit on fire. She fell back away from it with a yelp, landing on her backside.

"What's yours?" Dorian asked as he held his own steaming cup of hot chocolate.

"Electricity," Borden reported. "And somehow, the weather."

Dorian raised a questioning eyebrow.

"Don't make him angry," I said, mysteriously.

Julie wadded up another piece of newspaper and placed it in the fireplace. She rubbed her hands together, and I noted the changed expression on her face. Faster and faster she rubbed them, until finally she snapped her fingers.

The paper burst into flames.

With a triumphant look, she turned to me and Borden.

"Very good," I said with a smile, proud that she'd finally got it. Though I hated that she'd accomplished it by tapping into an angry thought.

The door to the solarium opened, and I looked up to find Nathaniel standing in the doorway.

He looked so happy there, so proud to watch our class going on.

But his presence meant that it was past nine o'clock.

"That's good for today," I said. "You all did great. We will see you tomorrow."

They each gave a nod and said goodnight, chatting excitedly with each other as they left. "See you tomorrow," Borden said quietly as he walked toward the door.

"I think I'll join class tomorrow," I acknowledged to him. Tomorrow was Borden's class—self-defense.

Borden nodded. "Just a heads up, Olin said he will be joining us."

I gave a little sneer, but felt bad, because I didn't really have a reason to detest his presence so much.

"Good night," Nathaniel wished Borden as he stepped out.

Alone, Nathaniel closed the door and walked in to sit on the couch. He let out a big huff as he did, which made me smile. I came to sit on the couch beside him, my elbow propped on the back of it.

"Long day at the library?" I asked.

He chuckled. "I forget how intolerable some freshman can be," he said. "They've been partying and living the college life this first month, and now their first assignments are coming due, but most of the stock has been checked out by those who are on top of it. Some of them get really irritable and think it's my fault the library has no more copies."

I chuckled, even though I felt for him. "Only seven

more months, and you'll never have to step foot in that library again."

Nathaniel gave me this look that said, *come on, Margot*, you know me better than that. I just laughed.

"When did you first fall in love with the library?" I asked, settling in and getting comfortable.

Nathaniel leaned in toward me just a bit, and I loved it, because this felt normal. We'd talked about this before, that we needed to become friends. We'd jumped straight into a relationship before. Now we needed to back up and rebuild our foundation. And that was exactly what we were doing.

"I was ten," he said. "I'd just been moved into a new foster home, the last one before it was just group homes. They were nice enough people, but I never felt like I fit in with their other children. But they went to the library just down the street from their house once a week. I didn't think I liked to read before that. But there was nothing else for me to do there during that hour. So I picked up a book. It was a children's history book on Egypt. It talked about mummification and pyramids and their gods. I was pretty much hooked on history from that point forward."

"So it was the Egyptians that hooked you?" I teased, smiling. "Typical."

"Hey, it was the Russians soon after that," he said, laughing in return. "All that blood and gore and power was pretty fascinating to a ten-year-old."

"So that's where your savagery came from?" I asked, raising an eyebrow. "You learned it from Russian history."

Nathaniel just chuckled and leaned his head back on the couch, staring up at the ceiling. "I don't think I ever asked you. Why Latin?"

I leaned my head on the back of the couch, letting my eyes wander up to the ceiling as well. "I guess it was just kind of always there. My father was into history, my mother a linguist. Latin is sort of the culmination of both of those things. Plus, I just always thought it sounded beautiful. Actually, it always sounded magical to me. Like spells and witchcraft, and what twelve-year-old girl doesn't want to have power, at least a little bit?"

Nathaniel turned his head to look at me, a little smile on his face. "Perhaps your blood just always knew. Even at twelve, you were meant to be a witch."

I laughed. "We don't call ourselves that, remember? Witches get hunted. Mages are smarter and respected members of society."

He just chuckled again.

"Have you made plans for your birthday yet?" Nathaniel asked. "Only two more days."

My eyebrows raised in surprise. "Honestly, I totally forgot about it. You get to twenty, and suddenly it's not such a big deal."

I loved the lightness about Nathaniel right now. I loved how he was laughing and smiling, and the weight of the world was nowhere near his shoulders.

"Well, good," he said. "Maybe don't make too many plans that day."

My eyes slid over to meet his. "Why?"

He just smiled and shrugged.

And so I smiled and laughed and relished in the normality of the moment.

CHAPTER SEVENTEEN

NATHANIEL THREW ME A SURPRISE PARTY. WHICH wasn't much of a surprise, considering his warning. Nathaniel showed up at my dad's house at six and put a blindfold over my eyes. But I'd walked to my new house so many times, I knew exactly where we were going.

The moment I walked through the door, everyone jumped out and yelled *surprise*.

All of my favorite people were there. They were all family by this point. All of the mages. My father. This was my whole world, my life, gathered together in my home.

It was the best day I'd had in a very, very long time. Turning twenty turned out to be my favorite age.

And the house was coming along. Brent's team had pulled off all of the destroyed siding on the outside, and thankfully it was good news underneath. It was almost all salvageable. They were currently working to reinsulate the entire house, and there was a massive pile of new siding and brick sitting on the front lawn.

All the floors were now sturdy and didn't even creak. I was told the new plaster was going to be installed in two weeks, and that was the part that I was really looking forward to.

Six months, and it would be a home I could live in.

On a rainy day at the very beginning of October, I sat in the solarium, waiting for the students to arrive for another history lesson. I read through one of the many journals we'd collected over the past year. This one was written by the hand of one Eta McDowens, who had fled to the United States after her parents were killed for being witches back in Scotland. She'd settled in Boston, and when the Salem Witch Trials began, she began talking about moving somewhere else. The journal ended before she said where.

Considering my mother had found this journal at a used book store in Boston, I had to assume this journal had gotten lost or forgotten.

The door to the solarium opened. I didn't look up until I finished the end of the page, but to my surprise, it wasn't Borden when I looked up, but Olin.

"Interesting reading material?" he asked as he walked in and sat in the desk chair.

"It's a journal," I said. "One of the mages who came from Scotland."

Olin shook his head and his eyes scanned the books on Nathaniel's shelves. "I admit, I cannot understand it. You and Nathaniel and Borden's fixation on the past. You live in such a spectacular time. Why go back and dwell on times that were so dark for our kind?"

My stomach knotted. "We just want to understand where we come from. The past gets repeated if you don't understand it. Isn't it better to learn from past mistakes so we can make a better tomorrow?"

An iron paperweight lifted from Nathaniel's desk, and I watched Olin's fixated gaze on it. Metals were his affinity. It was just a metal ball with a flat bottom. But under Olin's concentrated gaze, it changed shape. First into a beautiful, detailed rose. And then it rounded and elongated, transforming into a snake.

"If you think the past holds all the answers you're looking for, I think you are wrong," he said. The snake curled up in on itself, looking tortured. Slowly it bloated and rounded, and suddenly, it was just a ball of iron again. "The past was not like your times. They were not connected. They did not travel. Certain areas knew how to do certain kinds of magic, but there was not a cross-sharing of abilities or knowledge. People have always been suspicious of one another when it comes to strangers. The mages were no different, Margot."

What he said made me pause. Why wouldn't that be true? It was the case in every other aspect of history. Why would it be any different when it came to those who could wield magic?

"Then that is our mission," I said. "To gather up all the knowledge from the past. To further the study. To be smarter. To take what they knew and share it with all of us."

"And that," Olin said as a small smile started to grow on his face, "that is a worthy use of our time."

The door opened, and in stepped John, followed by Marie and Julie.

"Enjoy your history class," Olin said as he stood, giving the students a smile. Without another word, he walked out the door, passing Borden on his way out.

Borden met my eyes, holding them for a long moment. "Everything alright?"

I paused for just a moment in giving my answer. "It's fine," I said.

Except, when I walked into the solarium two days later to teach my healing class, I found all four of my students, and Poppy sitting with Olin.

I paused in the doorway since no one had seen or heard me yet.

"One way of thinking sounds like tyranny, doesn't it?" Olin asked them.

"You can say that," Dorian said. "But that doesn't

make it true. Tyranny is when you don't let anyone have a choice."

"Then would you call it manipulation?" Olin asked. "Because when you are tricked into one way of thinking, what else can it be?"

"I'm not sure what you're trying to do here, Olin," Poppy said, speaking up. "Are you trying to create contention? Because it sure feels like it."

Olin shook his head. "Not at all. I simply believe that every person should think about things in every direction. An open mind is an enlightened mind. Do not ever let anyone do your thinking for you, simply because it seems like they are doing the right thing."

They all paused at that, seeming to mull it over.

So I chose to step into the room at that moment. "He's right. We do all need to think for ourselves. With all the facts in hand, with our own research done, we can make wise decisions."

Olin looked up at me with an expression I couldn't quite read. The others looked a little guilty, like they'd been doing something they shouldn't have.

I didn't like that they felt like that.

"Every single person here is free to discuss whatever they like," I said, setting down the books I planned to cover today. "Playing devil's advocate is never a bad thing, so long as you've thought through things. If there is anything you'd like to discuss, I'm happy to dive into it."

And I felt a little better when each of my students

met my eyes with confidence, and they each shook their heads.

"Olin, would you care to join us for our lesson today?" I asked.

He stood, aiming for the door. "I think I'll pass today. I think I have the healing part covered."

I watched through the glass as he walked out and down the garden path.

"I don't know if I like him very much," Poppy said. "Some people seem drawn to drama. I'd say he's one of those kinds of people."

The others muttered words of agreement.

I swallowed once, trying to decide what, if anything, should be done about the situation.

But I had a task at hand. So I turned back to my students, and we began our lesson.

CHAPTER EIGHTEEN

"I finished the translation on the French book," Nathaniel said.

I turned, watching him walk from the bedroom into the living room that would one day be grand again. "Oh?"

He held a mischievous smile as he walked to my side, carrying a notebook.

"And?" I probed, knowing whatever he said, it was going to be good.

"It's an instruction book on how to turn any kind of food into chocolate."

I tried to keep a straight face because he was keeping a straight face. But I lasted about two seconds before I burst into laughter. Nathaniel couldn't hold it in any longer, either.

"I spent two entire weeks scouring France," I said,

wiping at my eyes because there were tears leaking from them. "And we found one book, in the entire country, and it's about chocolate?"

"What?" Nathaniel questioned. "You don't think chocolate at any time is worth the effort?"

I laughed again and shook my head. "I've got a box of crackers up in the office. Should we at least give it a try?"

"Seems like a terrible waste if we don't," he said, and I loved the smile that had returned to his face whenever we were together anymore.

"Be right back," I said. And I darted up the stairs, taking them two at a time. I wound my way up the spiral staircase, snatched the box from my desk, and made my way back down.

I followed Nathaniel outside, and that felt like extending an olive branch. He knew how much I loved being out in the sun, down by the beach. And we were enjoying the last few days of warmth before fall took complete control and dipped the temperatures.

The process for transforming food into chocolate was more complicated than I expected it to be. It was a combination of transfiguration and an expression of love, and then a funny hand movement that felt like we were trying to create a snowball, with the food held between your hands.

But when I opened them again, what had once been a wheat cracker, now looked exactly like chocolate.

I looked up at Nathaniel with wide, shocked eyes.

He stared at me the same, his own chocolate in his hands.

"That's actually amazing," I said. And I put the chocolate into my mouth. I bit down into it, and the creamy, chocolate taste exploded in my mouth. "This… this is the best chocolate I've ever had in my entire life."

"It really is incredible," Nathaniel said in wonder as he slowly chewed. "This…" He chewed a little more. "Margot, I have to say, it was worth your two weeks of searching, and these two weeks of translating."

"Absolutely," I said, my brows raising as I nodded in agreement. "This…this could be a problem. I think I may just end up gaining twenty pounds in the next month because all I will ever want to eat is chocolate."

Nathaniel shook his head. "Not true. The human body has its limits with how much chocolate it can withstand."

"Do tell," I said as I popped the other half of the chocolate into my mouth.

Nathaniel licked his fingers off, then pulled his knees up to his chest and wrapped his arms around them. "There was this group home I was in, when I was about thirteen. Stingy as could be when it came to food. Not a single one of us had an ounce of fat on our bodies to spare. So one night, I was so hungry, I wandered out and broke into the kitchen. They had this entire bin of chocolate chips. Not that they'd ever made anything for us with them. But I sat on the floor of that pantry and ate chocolate all night. But the next morning, I was so sick I thought my insides would turn out, I threw up so much. I didn't like chocolate much for about a year after that. Besides, I got caught and sent to their version of solitary for two entire weeks."

I shook my head. A heavy sigh made its way out of my lips then and I leaned back, laying in the sand. "The system is so terrible," I said. "You should never have had to worry about having enough to eat."

"The story was about chocolate, Margot," Nathaniel pointed out. "Not a pity party."

He laid back too, and across the sand, I found his hand and laced our fingers together.

"What does it take?" I asked. "For us to actually be together again? Is there some kind of trigger or event that needs to take place?"

"We still haven't really figured anything out yet," Nathaniel pointed out, again, being logical and clear. "And we haven't really been trying very hard."

I shook my head. "We've been doing other important things," I said. "Like this. Talking. Being real. Explaining our past."

Nathaniel turned his head to look at me, and I turned mine to look at him in return. "I feel like things are different now. You went away for a few months, and now you own a house, and I'm a senior and student teaching, and teaching mage classes. I feel like we're in very different places than we were before."

I nodded, because I absolutely agreed. "Does this mean we're adults now?" I asked, making both of us smile a little.

"I think maybe we might be," Nathaniel said. And his smile was my favorite thing in the world.

"Maybe this means our problems are different now, and what caused the problems before won't be the same problems," I said, my heart beating a little faster.

Because it was true. All of our problems before circled back to the Society Boys. Their bullying and causing problems for Nathaniel and me and Borden, was what tore us apart.

But those Boys were long gone. We would never see them again.

And maybe Nathaniel was right. Waiting them out had made the problem go away. And what good did my confrontation with them do?

"It's already starting to feel like a distant memory," Nathaniel said. He reached up and brushed his knuckles over my cheek.

I reached up and pressed his palm against my face, relishing in the feeling of his touch. "And maybe we can go into this better this time. Building our friendship. Our grounding. And we walk into this, one sure step at a time."

Nathaniel propped himself up on one elbow, looking down at me. "I think this is a brilliant plan."

I smiled, and Nathaniel smiled, and everything in the

world felt right once more as he leaned down. One of my hands rose to lace my fingers into his hair.

And he kissed me. It was so calm and confident. So easy and gentle.

But it reached down into the pit of my stomach and took hold. It sent shots of electricity out to my toes, my fingers.

I still didn't know if we were together in any kind of official way. But it didn't even matter. Because there was no one else, and there never would be anyone else.

Nathaniel held my heart, and that was never going to change.

CHAPTER NINETEEN

The following day, I walked back from the post office with a heavy feeling in the pit of my stomach.

We had found two different people to do the German translations for us. We'd found another to do the Swiss translations. So last night, Nathaniel and I had spent an hour enchanting the books with everything we could think of, everything we could make up, to protect them. We filled their pages with forgetfulness, so that hopefully, the translators would forget what they'd translated as soon as they walked away from the books. We made it so that no one could even think about sharing the books or the translations with anyone else.

We had no idea if any of it would work one little bit, but we had tried, and now we had to trust in our abilities. While Nathaniel was at school and everyone else was busy with one thing or another, I took the books into the post office. I'd carefully packaged them up with a note to each translator. And then I felt sick as the postal worker took the boxes and put them in a big bin with a mound of other packages to be sorted and then mailed.

Afterward, I'd gone to the jewelers and sold more gold. And then I had to make him forget that I'd been in there so many times lately.

Raising the funds to fix the house wasn't cheap. I was spending as much money to fix the house as I had to purchase it.

I walked up the stairs to my father's house and let myself in.

Funny how quickly I had started to separate it. It wasn't my house, even though I had lived here my entire life. This was now Dad's house, and the one down on the beach was mine.

Was I being prideful?

I didn't think so. I should be proud.

I was a twenty-year-old woman, who had taken control of her future and executed her plan to make it happen.

As always, there were stacks of books all over the house. Dad had finished another last night and left it on the little table between his and Mom's chairs. There was a stack of history books sitting on the floor next to it, and I wondered if they were teaching material, or for fun. You could never tell with Dad.

I smiled as I walked upstairs and went to my bedroom.

Like everywhere else in the house, my walls were lined with books. Fairy tales and children's books from my youth. School books and textbooks I certainly didn't need any longer.

But I had rearranged the shelves over the last year. Now, the one in the middle held all books pertaining to magic.

My eyes lingered on the books on the middle shelf. They were the ones we'd found in my mother's secret office. I thought of her, going through so much effort in scouring the New England area, searching by hand and eye to find books having to do with magic.

The number of books we'd found as a team was nearly tenfold. And done in a much shorter span of time.

I wished she could be here to see what we'd done. I wished we could share our knowledge with her, and her with us.

She'll find her way back someday, I thought to myself.

I had two hours until Borden and I were going to meet up and work on the weaponry book I'd found in the Foster room back at Alderidge. Even if it didn't feel particularly applicable, I didn't want us wasting any time. We had endless learning still to do.

So while I had time, I scanned the shelves.

I'd finished Eta's journal. So I picked up the next one.

The handwriting in this one was a little rougher,

making me wonder if perhaps the author was a bit younger. It was written in English, and by the way it was worded, my guess was that this individual was from England.

I skimmed it quickly, looking for a name. And at the very end of it, it was signed Katherine Dowdle.

Her life, as recorded, was simple. She did chores. She talked about boys. She had a younger brother who drove her mad. Her mother was expecting another baby, a late surprise that had them all worried for her health.

But she started talking about the family meetings. How all of her aunts and uncles and cousins would gather at their grandparents' home to teach the children. They were taught levitation and weather control. They were taught invisibility and history. From one elder to the next, they passed down their knowledge.

As she got older, her thoughts grew more pensive. She talked about the witch trials that happened in the past and how angry they made her. She spoke of the injustice and voiced her concern to her family.

They all brushed her aside. Told her to keep her head down and to conceal her magic whenever possible.

She didn't want to conceal her magic. She didn't want to live in fear.

My heart started pounding harder as I read familiar sounding words.

Fear. Why did some of us have to believe it was only about fear?

A knock at the door sent my stomach up into my throat. When I heard it open downstairs, I looked up at the clock. It was already time.

I heard footsteps on the stairs, then Borden knocked on my open door and walked in. I knew what we were going to be working on today, but I was still shocked when he held a full-on sheathed sword in his right hand, and some kind of curved blade in his other.

"You're lucky you didn't get shot by a police officer walking over here holding those," I said, glaring at him for being so careless.

"Streets are dead right now," he said, laying the weapons on my bed and taking a seat on the edge of it. "Everyone's at school or work right now. I doubt anyone saw me."

My eyes shifted back to the journal that laid open on the desk. "Do you think we're controlling everyone with fear tactics?"

Borden followed my line of sight, landing on the journal. "You been talking to Olin again?"

I shook my head. "I've been reading another of the journals. This is from a young woman named Katherine Dowdle. She had a lot of thoughts and feelings on being taught to fear using her magic, fearing getting caught. Looks as if Olin isn't alone in his feelings."

Borden took a deep breath and shook his head. "Maybe it is fear. But it isn't unjust. I think no matter how powerful we become, we're always going to be vastly outnumbered. Unless we unleash something astronomical, we will never really be able to take over the whole world. So, that means we're always going to have to be careful."

"Exactly," I said, nodding. I let out a sigh. I hated that I was feeling like this. And I began to realize that this would always be a debate among our kind. It had been in the past, and it would continue to be in the future. "Anyway, I don't really want to talk about it anymore. You brought the book?"

Borden nodded and produced it from the pocket of his jacket.

Concealing weapons was not the easiest. It involved copying transfiguration, sort of like how we had glamoured the books to be unreadable to anyone but a mage. But it involved a surge of will. We worked on the sword first, and Borden grabbed my grandfather's old cane from a closet. It was black and gnarled with a snake carved into it. Really, it was gothic and grotesque, but also oddly a symbol of power.

Borden and I both said the words, which were in Latin. "Facere videntur periculo tutus donec redderet animam."

The sword we both held in our hands began to transform from the tip to the hilt. The flat edge rounded and a wood grain appeared in its surface. The hilt warped down, attaching to the shaft. And the shape of the snake began to take form.

And within sixty seconds, an exact replica of my grandfather's cane rested in both our hands.

Borden looked up at me, and the smile on his face excited me.

"That was amazing," I said in a breath. I let go, leaving it in Borden's hands. He stood it on end, resting his hands atop the head of the snake. Oddly, it was kind of a natural sight. Borden was a powerful man with a touch of his own darkness, and that snake cane looked oddly at home in his hands.

"Was your grandfather some kind of mobster?" Borden asked, testing the balance and weight of the cane. I wondered if it felt as heavy as the sword, even though it didn't look like it right now.

I laughed. "Not exactly," I said. "He was my mother's father, so he would have been a mage. But he was fascinated with science fiction and fantasy. His office was full of odd things. Skulls and old jewelry. Odd drawings, ancient mirrors. He loved that cane. Went everywhere with it as he got older and couldn't walk as well."

Borden gave a nod, and it was actually kind of entertaining how pleased he seemed with it. "Right. Let's see what it takes to bring it back to its true form."

It took him twenty minutes. Great beads of sweat started to form on his forehead as he swung it like a sword. He cursed as he thrust it forward. He closed his eyes in deep concentration and then thrust the tip of it into the ground.

And finally, as he swung it in my direction with a concentrated look on his face, it suddenly transformed from the cane, back into the sword.

Borden stopped it just two inches from my neck.

My eyes widened with fear and I stumbled back a step.

But Borden just smiled, and I realized I had never been in danger of being beheaded by him.

"It took the thought that I needed to defend myself," he said in conclusion. "That I had to fight for my life." He lowered the sword, and instantly, it melted back into the cane. "This…I hate to admit it, but I kind of enjoy this kind of magic, Margot."

I chuckled and shook my head, breathing out in relief. "You're such a boy. Boys and their wooden swords. Except this one transforms from wood into a real sword."

Borden grinned in mischief as the sword once more shifted back into a cane. He twirled it dramatically. "Your turn."

We transformed the curved blade into a strand of pearls with a pull release clasp. I'd judged Borden a little for how long it had taken him to get the cane to transform back into the sword. But it took me just as long.

And it finally worked when I got it in my mind that I truly had to defend myself. I swung through the air in Borden's direction, and suddenly I wasn't holding a strand of pearls anymore. It was the hilt of the blade.

"I think we need to add this to the second-semester self-defense class," Borden said, utterly pleased when we called it a day three hours later.

"You really think it's a good idea for any mage to run around with a deadly weapon accessible at any time?" I asked, because really, I wasn't so sure.

"Do you really not feel safer with those pearls around your neck right now, knowing how outnumbered you are?" he asked as he raised an eyebrow at me.

My lips spread into a thin line. He wasn't wrong. I did like the feeling of being able to defend myself at any moment. But again, where was the line between fear and normalcy? "I'll think about it."

I said it, even though I knew I didn't have the only say. I wasn't the queen of the mages.

From the smirk on Borden's face, I almost wondered if he could read my thoughts. "I think we should teach Nathaniel this when he has some free time. That boy is always getting into trouble."

He turned to leave, and I followed him to the front door. I noted that he took the concealed cane with him. "I can't disagree. Though I have no idea if he would ever, ever use it."

Borden shrugged. "But at least he will have the option. Goodnight, Margot."

"Night," I said, watching for a moment as he set off down the sidewalk.

I set to making dinner, knowing Dad would be home

in thirty minutes. I settled for shepherd's pie, in the mood for something homey and comforting.

It had five minutes left when Dad walked in and hung his scarf on the tree stand beside the door.

"How was your day?" I asked, folding my arms over my chest and leaning against the counter.

Dad walked into the kitchen and set his briefcase on the table. He pulled a chair out and plopped down in it, looking exhausted. "Good. Long though. I gave them all a quiz today, and let's just say it was very telling among the freshman."

I chuckled and shook my head. "Easy now. Remember, it hasn't been that long since I was among their ranks."

Dad smiled. "To be honest, that feels like ages ago. There are times I forget that you turned into a revenge gremlin and got yourself expelled."

I gave him a dark look, even with a smile curling on my lips. "Hey, now."

He just laughed. "Yet here you are. A homeowner. Starting your own curriculum. You were just in too much of a hurry. Got it all figured out and went and grew up on me."

"I'm still here for now," I said, smiling sadly because his mood was sobering. "And I'll always be your little girl. No matter what."

He offered me a smile and then the timer went off. I

pulled the food out of the oven, and my father and I had a wonderful meal together, talking and laughing. And everything in the world was normal for an entire hour.

CHAPTER TWENTY

I woke up early.

I wasn't sure why. But when I rolled over and looked at the clock on my nightstand, it said it was 5:12. And I was wide awake.

I rolled out of bed and quietly used the restroom, so I didn't wake Dad up, then padded my way back into my room. I grabbed Katherine's journal, crawled back into bed, and continued where I'd left off.

There was a concentration of mages in the next town over. And she heard there was a man there who believed like she did. That the mages should band together and come forward. That they should take their place in the world.

She traveled for three days. It took her another two days to track him down.

My scalp tingled as I read the name *Bealdor*. And for the first time, I had a last name. *Bealdor Rayburn.*

All the lines were connecting in our history, and I instantly remembered everything Otto had told Borden and I in Germany.

Katherine described Bealdor Rayburn as a man gaining power and influence. He spoke to her of being brave. Of setting an example to the other witches. He spoke to her of not living in fear.

He did not want to live as if they should be ashamed of being witches.

The more I read, the more my stomach tightened. The colder my hands got. The more something started ringing in my ears.

Katherine bought into everything he said. She believed in every way of thinking Bealdor Rayburn taught.

They made a plan. They would overtake the local lord who had led the recent witch hunts. They would make him pay, and they would gain the freedom of their people.

But they needed more bodies. Katherine returned to her family to convince them to join.

But everything fell apart. On their way to overthrow their local leader, Sandris and his people intercepted them. Bealdor Rayburn ran, half of her family lost their magic, and Katherine barely made it out with her life.

I will never live down the guilt and sorrow that

consumes my soul, Katherine recorded. *Because of me and my arrogance, my mother and my uncle are dead. My father and my sister have lost their magic forever, and now our entire clan must flee. Our lives are ruined because of me.*

Because I thought we needed glory and respect.

I cannot hide my shame far enough. But perhaps the Americas will be a start.

Her last journal entry was dated 1655, just one year before Sandris locked half of all magic.

It was tragic, reading how it all ended.

But my mind kept circling back around to Bealdor Rayburn.

This was the same man Otto Huber had told us about. The same man who launched half a dozen witch hunts, because he did not want to live in the shadows.

Something knocked on the back of my mind. A memory.

Rayburn. I knew that name, from somewhere. Something. Maybe something I'd read?

But Bealdor… Something about that word felt…off to me. It didn't actually sound like a name. I'd certainly never heard it before.

I stood and walked out my door, straight down the stairs and to one of the bookshelves along the staircase. My eyes scanned until I found the one I was looking for.

It was a book of translations, of Old English to modern English.

I darted back up to my bedroom and crawled onto

my bed. I opened the translation book, and skimmed as I reached the Bs, double checking the spelling from Katherine's journal.

B… Bealdor: Master.

Bealdor wasn't a man's name. It was a title. And likely not even a legal one at that, considering it was talking about a mage.

My heart thundered.

I was so close.

It was right on the tip of my tongue.

My gaze lost focus as I stared at a map on my wall.

And suddenly, my mind fell backward, to a crowded hotel room in Scotland. To Nathaniel speaking words written on a sealed book.

A man erupted from the book.

"What is your name, Sir?" Nathaniel had asked, with such kindness in his voice.

"Olin," he had responded. *"Olin Rayburn."*

"Oh my gosh," the words slipped over my lips in a breath as I dropped the journal.

We'd been so stupid. We'd hardly even questioned Olin. We were so desperate for there to be more of us, we'd just invited him in and brought him into the fold.

Olin was from England, the same area where there had been a cluster of witch hunts, hunts I now realized he pushed into action. He was always talking about not living in fear, how we could be so much more in the world.

He'd been trying to persuade my students.

He'd been trying to convince me and Nathaniel and Borden.

And suddenly, I realized all the lies he had told us.

When he first appeared out of the book and we asked him what year he thought it was, he'd told us 1656.

He'd said that he and his family worked for fifteen years trying to find a way to unlock magic.

The Lock of Sandris happened in 1656.

My hands rose to my hair, my fingers lacing back into it.

If he'd really spent fifteen years trying to unlock magic, he would have said it was 1671.

And Olin told us Sandris had obliterated himself locking magic. When he'd really survived, and didn't die until two months later.

We'd been so, so stupid. If we'd just taken ten seconds to think about his story, we would have instantly seen all the cracks.

And instantly, I had no doubt. Olin was Bealdor Rayburn, who caused the death of so many mages. Who was so selfish. The man who I now realized was locked into a book by Euan Sandris himself.

Sandris had been found dead, but with signs of a magical struggle. His body was devoid of any magic.

And suddenly I didn't doubt it. Sandris died and burned up the last of his magic locking Olin in a book.

Let him be locked away, until the world be prepared to grant him his due.

The words had been spelled out, right there on the sealed book.

And we'd thought nothing of it.

Rage flashed through my blood. Hot adrenaline spiked in my system, and I found myself at my closet, yanking on clothes. I ripped my hair back into a bun and stuffed my feet into shoes. I set out into the early morning fall air.

Olin had found a room to stay in on campus at one of the boys' housing units in exchange for upkeeping it. So with charged determination, I set out across the campus grounds in the direction of the house.

I was halfway there, when I saw a figure step out from the front door, taking out a bag of trash. He threw it in the bin, and then looked up, meeting my eyes.

Olin. Olin Rayburn. Bealdor. Master.

I stormed across the grass, feeling a charge zip through my blood. I felt the grass beneath my feet stand straight. I felt the dirt begin to tremble beneath my feet. I could swear, I was rallying every bit of earth and nature beneath me as I headed straight for him.

I slipped the coin from my pocket and brought my fist up to my lips. "I only want my family to be safe," I spoke the truth to the coin.

Olin looked at me warily, eyeing me as I approached.

I didn't hesitate as I walked up to him. "You need to

be honest with me about who you really are," I said, my voice nearly trembling with rage as I spoke.

A range of emotions swept over his face as I walked right up to him.

I held my hand out and he brought his up, his eyes dropping to it.

But just as I dropped the coin, he turned his palm, and it fell to the cement at our feet.

His eyes rose up to meet mine, and ice spread through my veins.

"Why were you really sealed into that book?" I asked. The tiny bits of dirt on the concrete trembled and began to lift into the air. "Who really sealed you into it?"

"Why so curious now, Margot?" Olin asked. He raised his chin, and as he did, I heard the gutters along the roof rattling.

"Because I know you haven't been honest with us," I said. Every hair along the back of my neck stood on end, and I felt something rising within myself and in the space surrounding. And that something felt like danger.

"I'm a simple man who just wants to be among those like him," he said. I noted the doorknob rattling now as well.

I shook my head. "I always felt like your views were dangerous for us. Tell me, Olin. Do you remember Katherine Dowdle, and what happened to her family?"

At her name, the expression on Olin's face went slightly slack. The color drained from it.

And the world exploded.

The gutters and the doorknobs tore themselves apart and I stepped back at the volley of metal shards. I wrapped an arm around my face in defense. And at the same time, a carpet of grass tore itself from the ground and wrapped in front of me, blocking the metal shards aimed for me.

I stepped back with a scream of violence stopping at the back of my teeth.

Olin stared at me with dark eyes that promised my demise.

I spread my hands out, feeling deep into the earth. And I brought up every baseball-sized rock that was hidden beneath the ground. They shot up from the grass, from the cement, and instantly pelted toward Olin.

He brought up his hands as well, and every bit of metal from every building around us came flying toward him in tiny bits, only to melt together instantly, forming a shield in front of him.

My rocks hit them with a thunderous noise and fell to the ground.

We were going to draw too much attention. We were causing so much noise. Any second now, there would be faces appearing in the windows.

I had to get us away from people.

I started backing across the lawn of the university, along the side of it, to the arch that led down to the beach.

"It didn't work before," I said as I walked back. Olin advanced, thinking I was afraid. "You got hundreds of people killed. Why would it be any different today?"

Olin's shield began to shred apart, and my eyes widened in horror as two dozen spears formed, all pointed directly at me. "We keep dancing in the same circle, Margot. I think, at this point, we're just going to have to agree that we're never going to find level ground between us."

A scream ripped from my chest as I held my hand out to one of the trees to my side, ripping it in its entirety from the ground and placing it between me and Olin, just as he launched the metal spears through the air at me.

He was going to kill me. Because I knew the truth now. Because he knew I would fight him, because I would get in his way, and I wouldn't be quiet.

Olin wanted to bring us all into the public view.

And he wasn't going to let me stand in the way of his vision.

The spears flew around the tree, sticking into the grass, others thudding into the tree I held suspended in front of me.

With a scream of anger, I launched the entire tree at Olin.

He yelled his own war cry, pulling more and more metal to him, which formed into a giant sword. It sliced clean through the entire tree. He advanced toward me between the two massive ends of the tree.

I turned now. I sprinted. I ran.

Eyes would turn our way. Perhaps they already had. They would see this battle of magic and we would be exposed, because too many people around here knew exactly who I was, and who I associated with.

I sprinted toward the beach.

New spears volleyed at me, and I screamed as one caught me in the shoulder, just as I dashed down onto the sandy beach.

I turned, throwing my hands out, sending a spray of sand at Olin, temporarily blinding him.

I gripped the sand as it surrounded Olin, wrapping him in it entirely.

With a grunt and a scream in my mouth, I lifted him straight into the air and aimed him out over the ocean.

I didn't want to do it, but I knew exactly where this was headed.

Olin would kill me. It was exactly what he was trying to do.

And now that I knew the truth of who he was, he wouldn't stop trying to kill me.

I had to stop him. And now I knew that the only way to do that was to put an end to him.

I felt myself growing hot inside. I felt this surge in my blood. And I felt all of my hair lift from my scalp as I clutched Olin in the sand, giving me control over his movements.

But I heard something in the distance. A voice.

I thought maybe I heard my name.

In that moment, my concentration slipped.

And I heard Olin shout words. Words I didn't understand.

And something black shot through the air from Olin to me.

It struck me in the chest.

I gasped for air.

I staggered forward, losing my concentration, and Olin dropped into the shallow waters.

That blackness seeped into my chest. It searched for my heart, and took hold of my lungs.

I couldn't breathe.

I clawed at my own chest, trying to get it out of me.

But it swept up to my eyes, and I could only gasp in horror, as my vision clouded and the blackness swept in.

I heard my name called once more, and I thought maybe it was Nathaniel.

But I couldn't tell. I collapsed forward, landing face first in the sand.

CHAPTER TWENTY-ONE

My mouth tasted like sand. My eyelids had surely been glued shut. My arms felt dead and my legs were unquestionably made of lead.

I turned my head, feeling an uncomfortably flat pillow beneath my neck.

I blinked my eyes open. They were the stickiest things in the world.

I saw bright windows, filled with sunlight. There was an ugly tan chair and to the left, I saw…medical equipment.

With a groan, I lifted my head and blinked three times.

I was lying in a bed, and I was wearing a hospital gown.

With another groan, I ground my hands to my head, because it felt like it was filled with cotton.

A gasp ripped my eyes to the door, and I looked to find a nurse pausing there.

"You're awake," she said in shock. She walked in and started checking my vitals, not even saying a word.

"Why am I here?" I asked, looking around in confusion. Something felt…off in my brain. Really, in my entire body, but I just felt like something had been twisted and muddled in my head.

"You collapsed and the doctors have been working tirelessly to figure out why," she said as she wrote my vitals down on my chart.

"Collapsed?" I asked. I couldn't remember what had happened. I didn't remember collapsing, or anything that would cause me to collapse.

The nurse just nodded, continuing to write down her notes. "You just relax, dear. I need to go make some phone calls now that you're awake."

I blinked in confusion but nodded.

It felt as if my brain were lagging five seconds behind and I didn't process words quite quickly enough.

The nurse left the room, closing the door to just a little crack, leaving me alone.

I laid my head back onto the flat pillow, staring up at the ceiling.

What did I remember last? I dug deep into my brain, trying to recall what had happened, what I remembered.

Borden had come over to the house. We'd worked on concealing the weapons. He'd done a…a sword, and made it look like a cane. I'd done... I shook my head, trying to recall what I'd done.

A blade.

I'd made them into a necklace of pearls.

I reached up to my neck, but of course they weren't there. I had nothing personal on. Not even my own underwear or bra.

I thought back again, trying to remember what happened after that.

I'd been in the middle of something when Borden showed up. I'd meant to go back to it when he left.

But for the life of me I could not think what I had been doing.

It felt important. But it wasn't there.

Just then, a doctor wearing a white coat walked in.

"Glad to see you awake, Miss Bell," he said. He grabbed a rolling stool from one corner of the room and took a seat, scooting over to my bedside. "I'm Dr. Griffin. Can you look into this light, please?"

He didn't give me a chance to say a word or react. He held up a small flashlight and blinded me with it, shining it directly into my eyes. He asked me to follow his finger, but with the light, it gave me a splitting headache. "Good," he said, despite how I felt. "Let's test this." He proceeded to test my reflexes. He looked into my throat. He peered into my ears. He felt my throat and pushed on my stomach.

My body felt strangely weak. I was tired from just a

few simple motions. It was difficult to stay sitting for very long.

"Why do I feel like this?" I asked.

But right then, my father walked in, followed immediately by Nathaniel.

And I got really, really worried by the expressions on their faces.

"I can't believe it," Dad said, immediately crossing to me and engulfing me in a hug. He squeezed so tight it actually hurt. "You're finally awake."

I met Nathaniel's eyes as I hugged Dad, and my dread deepened when I saw how bloodshot Nathaniel's eyes were, and moisture pooling there, threatening to spill down his face.

"What…" I asked, my brain still slow on the reactions. "What do you mean, finally? How long did I pass out for?"

Dad released me and cast a worried glance at the doctor.

"We didn't get a chance to discuss it yet," the doctor said. "Perhaps the two of you should tell her."

My stomach felt really cold, and it quickly spread throughout my entire body.

Nathaniel and Dad looked at me with this expression of dread and fear. But Nathaniel cleared his throat and took a step forward. He took both of my hands in his, and it took him a moment before he looked back up to meet my eyes.

"You collapsed on the beach," he said. "I was up on the shore, so I didn't really see what happened. But Olin was with you. He said you'd been practicing some magic from one of the books you'd found. It…it overwhelmed you. And you collapsed."

I blinked five times, trying to find this information, this memory in my brain. I tried to picture the ocean and Olin's face. I tried to remember what magic I'd been doing.

But the last thing I could remember was working on the weapons with Borden.

"I don't remember that," I said, shaking my head.

"It isn't uncommon in coma patients," the doctor said, and for the first time, I remembered he was here. Why he wasn't reacting to us talking about magic, I didn't know. Maybe Nathaniel or Borden had already messed with his head and made him forget any mention of anything unnatural. "To forget what happened leading up to the traumatic event."

My eyes slid back to Nathaniel's. "Coma."

He held my gaze, and I could tell, he didn't want to tell me this next part. "It's April thirteenth, Margot."

My heart dropped right down into the center of my stomach.

My mind whirled, trying to make this make any kind of sense.

No, it was only October. It was fall, the temperatures were turning.

I shook my head.

Nathaniel nodded his, that look of dread in his eyes. "You've been in that coma for six months, Margot."

I looked over at the doctor, because surely he would make all of this make sense. Surely he would correct Nathaniel and remind him that it had only been six hours or something.

But the doctor nodded. "We've been monitoring your vitals since you were brought in. We've been searching for what caused this, but as far as we could ever tell, you were perfectly healthy. So, we're exceptionally relieved that you're awake, Miss Bell."

Six months. Six months? I'd been asleep, lying in a hospital for *half a year*?

I'd missed Nathaniel's birthday. I'd missed Christmas and New Years. All of winter and half of spring now, I'd been in the hospital.

"Am…" my voice shook. "Am I okay now?"

The doctor looked down at my chart and shrugged. "Other than some muscle atrophy, you've appeared healthy this entire time. You're going to want to take it slow for several weeks. But I believe you can return home as soon as you are ready."

My brain couldn't keep up.

There were holes. My memory was missing pieces and I knew they were important.

But I couldn't find the pieces. I wasn't sure what to even look for.

So I sort of went into survival mode. People talked to me. The doctor ran more tests. Dad held up a bag, and there was something said about clothes.

Somehow I ended up dressed. And then we were checking out, and gently, my dad and Nathaniel helped me out of the hospital into undeniably spring air, and into the passenger seat of Dad's car.

I blinked, and we went from the hospital to Dad's house.

There was already a banner hung over our front door when I walked up to it. *Welcome Home* it said in big pink letters, in Poppy's handwriting.

When we walked inside, everyone was there. Borden and Poppy and Mary-Beth and Marie and Julie, Dorian, John and Olin. They cheered and were happy and expressed their excitement that I was home.

But it all felt a little overwhelming, because my brain was still lagging behind.

To them, I'd been asleep for six months. But to me, it was almost as if I blinked and woke up again. Time hadn't passed for me. I just had this gaping hole in my memory.

Thankfully, Nathaniel seemed to recognize how overwhelmed I was. After thirty minutes, he steered me out of the living room and up the stairs. He guided me into my bedroom and closed the door behind us.

I sat down on the bed, and stared at the floor until

that space filled with Nathaniel's face as he knelt in front of me.

I reached up and placed a hand along his face, and something inside of me relaxed just a little.

"It's okay if you're overwhelmed," he said as he mirrored my position. His hand against my face was so comforting. I leaned into it, breathing his scent in. "It's okay if you want to scream. It's okay if you want to ask a million questions tonight or if you just want to go to sleep. Whatever you need, Margot, it's okay."

It felt like there should be tears pooling in my eyes, because everything he was saying was what I wanted or needed. But I was just too tired for any of it.

"I just want to sleep for about fourteen hours," I confessed honestly. "But I don't want to be alone."

Giving me exactly what I needed, Nathaniel just nodded. He pulled back the blankets for me and tucked me in. And then he slid his shoes off by the door, and climbed into the bed with me. I laid my head on his chest and gently, his arms wrapped around me, holding me close.

I had questions. A lot of them.

But not tonight.

Tonight I just listened to the steady beat of Nathaniel's heart, the sound of his breathing. And both he and I fell asleep.

CHAPTER TWENTY-TWO

THE SUN WAS STREAMING THROUGH THE WINDOW when I woke up. It cast my entire room in a warm yellow glow.

I let out a sigh as I rolled over, feeling a little better now than I had yesterday.

And I felt even better when Nathaniel was there, face to face with me.

"How do you feel?" he asked as he reached up and brushed my hair out of my face.

"A little better," I responded, relaxing into the pillow. I studied his face, and it shocked me that I could see the time on his face, evidence of how much had passed. His hair had grown longer again and it curled around his ears just a little. There was at least three days worth of beard growth on his face, something I'd never really seen on him. His eyes looked a little more tired, and there was something a little more serious about the set of his lips.

"It really has been six months," I said as a statement.

Nathaniel's eyes dropped to mine and he nodded. His hand settled on my hip, and I loved the comfort here in this moment.

"That doesn't even seem real," I said, letting out a breath. "Six months is half a year. I must have missed a million things."

Nathaniel offered a sad little smile. "Would you like me to catch you up on everything?"

"Yes!" I stated, overly anxious.

Nathaniel let out a chuckle. "Well, we've sped up testing in the last two months. We've tested the entire school, we're sure of it."

"And…?" I asked.

He smiled again. "We found seven more mages, though only three of them aren't locked. We're waiting until after finals to tell them, though, and extend an invitation to the school. We thought it was unfair to distract them from their studies."

"And what's the plan after that?" I asked.

Nathaniel pulled in a breath and I could tell he was holding in excitement about whatever came next. "You talked about a trimester schedule. The first batch of students will be ready for their next semester in a few weeks. And this new wave will be ready. And your house…"

"My house!" I suddenly sat straight up in bed. I hadn't even thought about it until this moment. I scrambled out of the bed and started searching for clothes. "Is everything totally stalled? Did we run out of money? Has Brent walked away?"

Nathaniel swung his legs to the edge of the bed and sat there with a sheepish smile. And as I was pulling a sock on, I paused, waiting for his answers.

"There's been plenty of money," Nathaniel said. "Borden has been managing the fund disbursement. Brent has still been at work on the house. And it's very nearly finished."

All of my insides calmed and something fluttered up from the tip of my toes, up my chest, filling my arms, my brain.

I knew the smile on my face must be ridiculous.

"Would you like to go see it right now?" Nathaniel asked as his own smile grew on his face.

I could hardly speak. I simply nodded as I smiled like a lune.

Nathaniel held a hand out, and the moment I slipped mine into his, we were bounding for the door. I shrieked in pure joy as we jumped down all three of the front stairs and took off down the sidewalk at a run.

The air was crisp still, being the middle of April, but I could smell flowers in it. I could sense the earth coming back to life after its winter hibernation. I could feel the rising sense of new life, and it was exhilarating.

But I got exhausted just a dozen steps down the sidewalk, and I remembered that I'd been lying in a hospital bed for six months, my muscles dying a slow death.

Nathaniel didn't complain though. He slowed, and we walked together, hand in hand.

I felt happy. I leaned in closer, hugging myself to Nathaniel's side, and leaned my head against his shoulder.

He leaned down and pressed his lips to the top of my head. "That was the longest six months ever," he said against my hair. "I can't even imagine how it's been for you and your father, with your mother's disappearance. I still had you there, could still touch you. But not knowing what had happened…"

I shook my head, taking a deep breath. "I still can't remember what happened. What did Olin say we were doing?"

Nathaniel looked ahead and we turned down the road that would lead to my house. "He said you were practicing some kind of new levitation using the sand. Which, I could see. I had just stepped out onto the beach and saw you two. You were holding Olin up in the air, out over the ocean, surrounded by sand."

Some tiny little thing sparked in my memory. But it wasn't much. I'd been to the beach hundreds of times before. I had lots of memories there.

I shook my head. "The doctor said memory loss is normal. Maybe it will come back before too long."

"I'm sure it will," Nathaniel said, once more pressing a kiss to my head.

And my heart started thundering as we walked along the fence that surrounded the property the house sat on. I felt myself shaking all over in anticipation.

And then we stepped up to the gates, and my eyes widened with wonder.

The grounds, which had once been overgrown and dying, had been cleaned and manicured. Now there were clean, clear paths and a fresh driveway. There were beautiful plants, and the trees were defined and pruned. Off to the far right, I could see the pool house. It wasn't restored, as Brent and I agreed, but it had at least been cleaned and emptied.

And the house.

My whole heart surged.

Stark, brilliant white siding shone brightly in the sun. The beautiful brick work had been cleaned and restored. The new windows reflected the light and the stained-glass windows looked picturesque.

"You happy with it?" Nathaniel asked.

I had forgotten he was even there. With tears in my eyes, I nodded, filled to the brim with happiness.

"Come on," Nathaniel said taking my hand once more. "Let's go see the rest. Brent will be happy to see you."

The porch was in perfect condition as we walked up it. There were even two white rocking chairs on it and a few flowerpots that made me want to spend hours out here. The front door had been replaced with a big grand one, double-wide with stained glass windows at the top. I gripped the big brass doorknob and twisted it.

It didn't seem real that this was my house. That I owned this. It was mine.

But I walked right in, and tears finally broke free, sliding down my face.

The entryway was spectacular. The walls had been painted a sparkling white, and the floors had been repaired, sanded down, and refinished in a warm oak. There was a straight shot to the windows that looked out at the ocean.

"This is…" I said out loud in wonder as I walked past the parlor, which was beautiful, into the great room. The fireplace had been restored, the mantle refinished and stained. Four chandeliers were suspended from the ceiling, and the floors shone from the light.

My eyes shifted into the dining room adjacent.

There, just like I'd told Nathaniel I wanted, was a huge dining table that could seat fifteen people.

I just laughed in utter happiness and wonder.

And then I couldn't stop myself when I walked into the kitchen.

The cabinets were gorgeous. Polished oak and gleaming white countertops. A massive island was in the center of it, and there was the biggest stove I'd ever seen.

This was the kind of kitchen that could feed fifty people and not feel overrun.

"Is it all how you imagined?" Nathaniel asked.

I turned, and I couldn't contain my joy. I ran at him and jumped, looping my arms behind his neck and my legs around his hips. He caught me with ease, smiling at me. "It's even better."

I was done with this limbo of wondering. And I didn't question if anything had changed for him in the past six months.

I just kissed him.

I leaned my mouth down to his, bringing my hands to either side of his face, and I kissed him long and hard.

I let my tongue find his and I breathed in his breath.

This was how it was always meant to be.

Us. Together. In this house.

This was always meant to be our life.

Someone cleared their throat, and Nathaniel quickly set me down. I turned on a pirouette to find Brent standing there, blushing something fierce.

"Glad to see you up and awake, Miss Bell," he said, having a hard time meeting my eye. "Is, uh, is everything to your expectation?"

I took a step toward him, looking around as I shook my head in disbelief. "It's absolutely amazing, Brent. You've done a truly incredible job."

He smiled, and I could tell, he was proud of the work

he'd done. As he should be. "Would you like to see the rest of the house?"

I just nodded eagerly.

The bedrooms upstairs were very nearly finished. They needed carpet, which I was told was coming next week, and then the trim work would be finished. My office made me cry again, because it was so beautiful and spectacular. There was already a desk there, a gift from Borden, I was told.

Room after room, I imagined the students we could house and our teachers who could live here safely. This would be home. For nearly two dozen people, if needed.

And then Brent took us to the master bedroom.

Like the rest of the house, the walls were stark, brilliant white. The oak floors were shiny. The windows looked out over the ocean. And a giant chandelier hung from the ceiling.

"A giant bed with ten pillows, right?" Nathaniel asked to clarify. "And the fluffiest blanket I've ever seen?"

I smiled, remembering the request I'd made of him a long time ago. I nodded, leaning in, and kissed him quickly, so as not to embarrass Brent further.

"This is amazing," I said as we stepped into the bathroom.

There was a huge shower with brilliant blue tile running up the walls. Two big vanities were set up side-by-side. And the tub waited there, fully restored and beautiful.

"Can you imagine it a little more now?" I asked, running my finger along the edge of it. "Liking this tub?"

"I already like this tub, very much," Nathaniel said, and I relished every spark of hunger I saw in his eyes.

I smiled and winked, noting Brent had disappeared awfully quick.

Hand in hand, we walked back out into the great room, following Brent.

"It sounds like my friend Borden Stewart has kept up on keeping you paid?" I asked as we stalled in the entryway.

Brent nodded. "The man is good with money."

"He is," I agreed.

"We'll be completely finished here in two weeks and then you'll be clear to move in," Brent said. "Unless there's anything you see that you'd like changed or fixed?"

I shook my head. "All of it really does look wonderful. Thank you so much for taking such good care of my house while I've been laid up."

He just nodded. "Unless there's anything else, we're going to get finished up in that bathroom."

I smiled, and he walked off, back up the stairs.

Together, we walked back out and slowly made our way down the cobblestone path. "I cannot wait to move in," I said, smiling with wonder. "Are you excited?"

Nathaniel looked over at me, and I saw…a mix of feelings there.

"We have some talking to do, don't we?" I said. I kind of dreaded it, but I knew it was true.

"Yeah, we do," he said. "But it's been such a great day so far. It can wait till later."

I squeezed his hand in mine and felt a flutter of appreciation. And then something else dropped in my chest. "What day of the week is it?"

"Tuesday," he reported.

"Shouldn't you be in class?" I asked, the panic rising in my veins.

Nathaniel shrugged. "You're more important."

I stopped and looked up at him indignantly. "Nathaniel Nightingale! You're two weeks from graduating! You cannot afford to be missing classes right now!"

And that told me how much he loved me. Because this *was* important to him. Exceptionally so. And he was ditching a class to be here with me, helping me adjust to life after such a strange event.

I grabbed his hand, and together, we ran back down the street, all the way to Alderidge.

When we reached the sidewalk that led down to the main doors, we stopped.

I looped my hands behind his head and he set his hands on my hips. I looked up and up at his beautiful face. I loved our height difference.

"Now you go in there, and make all the other students look bad, because we all know you're the smartest man to pass through those doors in a generation."

"You make me feel a million miles tall," he said with a smirk of a smile as he gently pressed his lips to mine.

"That's because you are," I teased, nipping at his lip. "Now get going before you get in any trouble."

He quickly pressed his lips to mine and walked away.

I held onto his hand as long as I could, him looking over his shoulder.

And I smiled as I watched him bound down the sidewalk and then through the doors.

"Welcome back to the land of the living."

I turned to see Borden walking down the sidewalk. His hands were in his pockets, and he looked relaxed and…relieved.

"I'm still not convinced everyone isn't lying to me," I said. "Except that there are flowers blooming, and there's no more fall color."

We turned, and side by side, we walked together, no particular destination in mind.

"Trust me, it was the longest six months of my life," Borden said. And that sent a stone sinking into the pit of my stomach. "I was kind of hoping you could offer some answers as to what the hell happened, so none of us end up repeating it."

That sent a little wash of relief through me. "Trust me, if I could remember, I would tell you. But the last thing I actually remember was you and I enchanting the weapons. Then…nothing."

Borden shook his head. "That feels like ages ago."

"I'm probably really behind now, aren't I?" I asked, realization hitting me. "Have we gotten the translations back yet? What new things have you learned?"

Borden chuckled. "I think they're just about finishing up. Nathaniel has been handling all that. So, you haven't missed much of anything. Don't worry, Queen Margot."

I scoffed and glared at him. "Don't call me that. Besides, you're the one who has actual royal blood, Borden Stewart."

He just laughed, and then he treated me to breakfast.

CHAPTER TWENTY-THREE

I FELT LIKE ALL I DID WAS TALK UNTIL I WAS BLUE IN the face, repeating all of the information from my end. And played catch up.

Mary-Beth had taken it upon herself to draft the letters that would be sent out to our three new students. She had them sealed, and with only three days before school ended, she sent them, timing them to arrive on the last day.

My students were now as good at their subjects as I was, thanks to Borden and Nathaniel's careful instruction.

Poppy was coming along by leaps and bounds, and just before the semester ended, we got a phone call from her, saying that she'd found another mage on her flight from Paris to London. She'd spoken to him, believed he was a good person, and told him what he was. He was returning with her in a week.

Life was moving on, and it had carried on without me.

I actually felt relieved. At times I felt as if Nathaniel and I carried the weight of our world upon our shoulders. But we were growing. This was expanding, and none of us had to carry it alone.

The end of April arrived, and with it, came Nathaniel's graduation.

I walked to the solarium early that morning, carrying a basket of his favorite lemon poppyseed muffins and a jug of chocolate milk. I couldn't help but smile as I walked down the overgrown path. He usually tended this part of the garden, but with how busy he was these days, it had gotten overgrown.

I let myself in through the door, and stopped short when I stepped inside.

Nathaniel looked up at me from beneath his cap, dressed in his impressive gown. Two gold cords were looped behind his neck as well as a golden metal, a visible sign of the incredible work he had put in during his time at Alderidge.

He blushed sheepishly at me, but I just smiled in appreciation.

"I think I could get used to this look," I said, slowly walking forward, setting the basket on his desk.

"This graduate look does something for you?" he taunted me, lifting his chin a bit.

I bit my lower lip and proceeded forward. I reached out, resting my hands on his hips. Nathaniel reached out, hooking one finger under my chin, raising my lips. And like he owned them, because he did, he leaned down and pressed his lips to mine.

There were a lot of things I wanted to do in that moment. Like rip that gown off and anything that was underneath it. Like shove him back on his desk and climb him. Like let my lips trace a path from his own lips, down to unexplored territory.

But this was a big day, and there was no time to waste.

I pressed my lips hard to his once more before stepping away.

"Eat your breakfast," I commanded. "I made them special this morning. Then we need to get going."

"Yes, ma'am," he said, and I loved the turned-on tone he used.

I just smiled as I looked over my shoulder and saw Nathaniel grab one of the muffins roughly from the basket, and bite into it with vigor.

"So are you two back together officially, or what?"

Mary-Beth said the words in what I think she

thought was a whisper, but no one had a louder whisper than her.

We all sat together in the auditorium. Me, Mary-Beth, Borden, Dad, and Olin. There was a stage in the middle of the auditorium and Dean Lowell was handing out diplomas. Speeches had already been given. The school song had been sung. And now we listened as name after name was read off.

It was incredibly boring.

"Does it matter?" I whispered back to her, but I knew the others could hear me.

"Yes, it matters!" she said, all too loud. "It's kind of confusing these days. You're holding hands and kissing but no one has spelled things out. As far as I know, neither of you has worked out your very stupid issues that you broke up over in the first place. So, are you like, together, together, or is this just hooking up? Because the two of those could produce very different futures."

Someone *shhh'd* Mary-Beth from behind, for which I was grateful. I didn't want to answer her question.

She was right. Nathaniel and I did need to talk. We needed to pinpoint what was happening between us because, as Mary-Beth pointed out, it affected the future. We needed to see if we'd sorted through our issues. We needed to know if we could really move on.

I knew the answer in my heart, but we had to be grown-ups and talk it out.

I glanced at Borden out of the corner of my eye. But he just sat slouched in his seat, watching the commencement happening down below.

I hated that I felt this way. But it was there. Because I knew the feelings were real. Borden cared for me on a higher level. He'd told me he loved me. And I knew that if the circumstances were different, we could have become something.

But my heart was decided and I wasn't looking back.

Which left my feelings in this weird place. Because I couldn't lose Borden as a friend.

And it was just me being weird about it. Borden was acting like nothing had ever been confessed. He was simply being my friend. Which was exactly what I wanted.

I just didn't trust that it could be so easy.

Name after name was called. We reached the Ks. Then the Ls. Then the Ms.

And finally, the Ns.

"Patricia Nathans," a female voice called out. And then finally, "Nathaniel Nightingale."

We all stood up and whooped and screamed as Nathaniel rose from his seat and walked across the stage. He looked up at us, smiling and waving.

I pressed my hands to my mouth, pressing a kiss to them, and then waved my hands in his direction.

He acted as if he snatched something out of the air

and pressed it to his own mouth. He winked at me, and I felt myself blush.

Mary-Beth just shook her head at me. I ignored her.

Nathaniel waved to everyone else, beaming with joy for all the world to see, and my chest swelled with pride for him.

I might have decided finishing my college degree wasn't necessary for me, but Nathaniel had worked so hard for this. He'd turned his whole life around as a teenager for this. And here he was, receiving his degree in history with honors in linguistics.

I was so proud of him.

"Good work, Nathaniel!" Dad called out, and it made me even happier seeing the look on Dad's face as he clapped and cheered with all my friends. Nathaniel was like a son to my father. He loved that boy. And Nathaniel needed it. He had no family of his own anymore. They'd abandoned him when he was only three years old.

We'd made our own family for him.

THAT NIGHT, we all headed for the house. It still needed a name, but for now, it was just the house. Dad drove me in the car, with the groceries loaded in the back seat next to Nathaniel. Together, we each grabbed three bags and headed inside.

I'd put Mary-Beth in charge of decorations. I guess what resulted from that was really my fault.

My house was big. It easily qualified as a mansion. So the fact that it was almost completely filled with purple and silver balloons, Alderidge's colors, was impressive.

There were streamers hanging from every surface.

There was a huge banner that read CONGRATULATIONS, NATHANIEL hanging in the entryway.

The moment Nathaniel walked in, the commencement song started playing loudly from the record player, turned up as loud as it could go.

"You did it!" Mary-Beth shouted as she jumped around the corner, throwing her hands up in the air.

All three of us jumped violently.

"Congratulations on sticking it out and becoming the biggest smarty-pants in our already too smarty-pants group," she said as she bounded forward and wrapped her arms around Nathaniel in a very Mary-Beth hug.

"Thank you," Nathaniel said with a chuckle, hugging her back. "Nice work on the decorating."

"I knew you'd appreciate it," she said with a grin as she stepped back. She winked at me.

Someone changed the music. And we danced as we cooked dinner. We sang at the top of our lungs. We laughed and told stories, and we talked about the future.

We were all together. All the mages, minus Poppy, who wasn't due back with her newfound mage until tomorrow. But this was a preview of what would become the normal. In three days, Brent would be done with the last of the renovations, and I could move in full time. We could make this place a home. We could be together every day, and we could be ourselves.

We could do magic whenever we wanted. Just like right now, as someone had the dishes automatically washing in the sink. As someone changed the record without lifting a finger. As someone else made the chocolate-covered strawberries multiply so there were two dozen more on the platter.

This was going to be our life.

It was the perfect night.

As the hour crept toward ten, I headed for the door out onto the back deck, needing some fresh air. I opened the French doors, leaving them open, and stepped out to lean against the railing.

The air was still cool, but edging toward warm. I could smell the ocean, the tide was low, exposing a bigger expanse of sand. The night was calm and not a single wave crashed on the shore.

I leaned my forearms against the railing and looked out into the night.

Someone laughed inside, and another followed it, jovial and piercing. Olin said something in response to the joke, and the others laughed as well.

That tone.

My chin lifted.

Olin's voice.

"*Why so curious now, Margot?*"

I stood straighter.

"I'm a simple man who just wants to be among those like him."

I turned, looking back inside.

Olin stood there, talking to Dorian, smiling, and acting normal.

"We keep dancing in the same circle, Margot. I think at this point we're just going to have to agree that we're never going to find level ground between us."

My brows furrowed, and for the first time in weeks, that cotton inside my brain began to unwind.

Olin and I out on the lawn at Alderidge.

Us at the beach.

Me in my bedroom, reading a book.

No. A journal.

Bealdor Rayburn. Master Rayburn.

The people killed. The manipulation. His dangerous views that ended with thousands of people killed.

I squared my shoulders to Olin.

And it all came flooding back at once. Every single detail.

I lifted a hand, and all at once, a flood of sand rose from the beach outside and rushed past me. Before anyone could even blink, it wrapped around Olin's body and he rose three feet in the air.

"Margot!" someone yelled as I walked back inside, my gaze fixed on Olin, death radiating from my eyes.

"Margot, what are you doing?" Nathaniel asked with alarm in his voice.

But Olin squirmed in my grip. I anticipated it though, and tightened the sand around him, fixing his hands in place.

"It was him," I said, never once looking away. "Bealdor Rayburn. It was him. All the persuasion he's been trying to use. He's done it before. He launched half a dozen witch hunts. Hundreds of us are dead because of him."

"Margot, you don't—" Olin began to lie.

"I didn't pass out on the beach," I said, turning and walking Olin from the great room, out onto the deck. The others followed nervously, still not understanding what was going on. "I found out the truth and confronted him. He tried to kill me. And when you caught him, Nathaniel, he tried to act as if nothing happened."

"He tried to tamper with your memory," Borden said, and I appreciated that I could hear the decision in his voice.

"That's why you've felt so off since you woke up," Nathaniel said, and finally, he didn't question anything.

Olin laughed. Deep and dark, it started in his chest and worked its way up his throat, sending a wave of goosebumps flashing across my skin. "It's been entertaining, and surprisingly educational, spending time with you," he said. And suddenly my extended hand felt cold. It crept up my arm. "But you all are still such children."

A flash of cold instantly shot up my arm, and with a yelp, I lost my grip on him.

He and all the sand crashed to the beach.

I could have sworn I just blinked. Olin was fifteen feet from me. And then it was like the lights flickered and he was ten feet. Another flicker, and he was five. And with one more, the entire sequence happening in a flash of two seconds, he was on me.

I went down hard on the deck as Olin collided with me. I could hardly even think or move or breathe, and then his hands were around my neck.

His hands were ice cold. The coldest feeling in the world. It was so cold it felt hot and a scream erupted from my chest, only to be cut off at my throat.

Olin ripped away from me with a blast, and instantly thunder sounded overhead.

Just as the first raindrop fell, Nathaniel sprang through the air.

I barely scrambled into a sitting position in time to see him literally pounce on Olin.

Nathaniel's fists were swinging and they connected, blow after blow, with Olin's face. His chest. His ears. Olin reached for Nathaniel's throat, but Nathaniel rolled, coming on top of Olin's chest with a knee, holding him down in the sand.

Nathaniel didn't stop hitting him.

There was a savage, wild look in Nathaniel's eyes.

Olin's skin split, and suddenly there was blood on Nathaniel's hands.

And I understood then. Why Nathaniel was so non-confrontational now. This. *This* was what he was keeping locked up.

I saw it in his eyes, in his expression, in the adept way he fought: he could kill Olin. Nathaniel might be lean and wasn't nearly as built as even Borden was. But he was feral. He'd been brought up to survive. To be the last man standing, no matter the cost.

"Nathaniel!" I called out, even though I didn't know what I wanted him to do.

But it all shifted, because in a blink, Olin muttered words, and suddenly he dropped through the sand.

I blinked, unsure of what I'd just seen.

And suddenly there Olin was, standing in the shallow water, illuminated by a bolt of lightning.

We got half a second to react.

Olin outstretched his hands, and suddenly, hundreds of objects rose up from the beach, lost metal items. They instantly reshaped.

And he launched them at us.

We each reacted differently to defend ourselves.

I raised a wall of sand, knocking the metal shrapnel upwards as much as possible.

Borden instantly called a wave of rain that came pelting down, slowing their path.

Dorian threw up a shield of air. Marie sparked flames in her hands, ready to throw them.

A scream ripped from my chest as I held my hands out and called upon the ocean. I drew it up, creating a wave.

To my side, I saw Borden's eyes alight in that strange, white glow.

Another bolt of lightning cracked the sky.

It was as if it all happened in slow motion.

Olin stared at us with fixed eyes. And I saw all the history in them. All the selfish desires of his heart. The lives he'd gambled with. I saw promises that he would find a way. That he would do what he'd set out to do.

He raised his hands, and with magic I'd never witnessed before, a green disk glowed around each of them, filled with runes and ancient words I could not read.

"This is not over, Margot Bell," he said, clear as day.

He clapped his hands together and as he drew them apart, this…circular window opened. And there, I could see ancient buildings and clear blue skies.

Just as the lightning struck where Olin was standing, he stepped forward, through that window, and then was instantly gone, the window with him.

The crack of the lightning was deafening and the electricity that crackled through the air was suffocating. Each of us was thrown back, landing in the sand or on the deck.

My ears rang so loudly, I couldn't hear anything else, and I felt blind for a moment from the brilliance of the lightning.

"Margot!" I could hear my name being called, but it sounded muffled and far away.

I blinked, rolling to my side before getting to my hands and knees. As my vision slowly faded from blinding white to normal, I found Nathaniel in front of me, helping me get to my feet.

I stared at him, open-mouthed, in shock, over everything that had just happened.

There were sprays of blood over his face. It coated his white button up shirt. It was smeared all over his knuckles and hands. His hair was wild, and the look in his eyes was still… I'd never seen this Nathaniel before.

"Hold still," he said. And he held his hands up, hovering them over my neck.

And I didn't realize the searing pain my skin was under until it started easing away. A cry of agony came up my throat and I gripped onto Nathaniel's arms to keep myself upright.

Suddenly, strong arms wrapped around me as my father supported me from behind.

"Let's get her inside," Borden's voice made their way into my ears and then his face was in my vision. His eyes still glowed brilliant white, and the storm continued to rage all around us.

I didn't want to be weak, but I could hardly keep myself upright, so I let myself fall back into my father's arms, and Dorian took my feet. Nathaniel never moved his hand as he continued to heal whatever damage Olin had done.

They laid me on the couch, and slowly, Nathaniel's magic worked its way into my wounds from Olin's freezing hands. Slowly I could breathe easier. Slowly, the pain began to subside.

And when I felt normal once more, I sat up.

And I explained everything. All the lies Olin had told. All the truth I had discovered.

It was nearing midnight by the time I was done. Everyone sat listening with rapt attention. The mood was serious. Somber. Heavier than I'd ever felt in my entire life.

"He used portal magic," Mary-Beth said. "You realize that, right? The magic we've all been too afraid to even look at because of what happened to Margot's mom. Olin has been studying the book and practicing it, right under our noses."

"He could be anywhere now," Julie pointed out.

The look on Dad's face was grave. He was stone white and wouldn't let go of my hand.

"He's been sitting here among us for nearly a year now," Borden said. His eyes had yet to calm and return to their normal color. They still glowed brilliant white.

"We've been teaching him more magic, giving him more power and knowledge."

I shook my head as a thought sent my stomach sinking. "He knows more than we realize. When we fought before, we tore Alderidge up. I mean, I was tearing grass up and pulling trees from the ground. And he was throwing metal around and cutting through everything. People should have noticed. We weren't being careful. So how did he go and fix all that? Cover it up?" My stomach gave another twist. How had he done it? And the fact that he had altered my memories, when I was also a mage? "Olin is dangerous."

"And we never questioned his loyalty," Borden said darkly.

"He is one of us," John said. "We should have been able to trust him."

Nathaniel shook his head. "We got played like fools, because we were desperate," he said. Even his voice sounded different now. "And now he is out there, with more tools and more knowledge. And it's our fault. Olin is not going to give up his mission. He's held on to it for over three hundred years. He'll do whatever he can to recruit others to his way of thinking, and he will eventually try to expose us, just to bring us into the light and do what he wants."

Nathaniel looked over at me, and I saw how his carefully built walls had crumbled. This was a new man.

This was the forging of his two past selves, and I knew this was a new hybrid.

"We have to find Olin Rayburn," he said. And it amazed me how his voice now filled the room. How he now spoke with a new kind of confidence. "And we have to kill him."

CHAPTER TWENTY-FOUR

THE FOLLOWING TWO DAYS WERE SOMBER. THEY should have been filled with joy and excitement. Nathaniel had graduated university, the top of his class. My house was wrapping up. The first of May brought with it unseasonably warm weather, and it felt like summer.

But one of our own had betrayed us.

He'd tried to kill me.

And now we had no idea where in the world he'd gone. We had no idea how to find him.

"We have to live in the moment, you know?" Mary-Beth said as she helped me pack up the last of my things in my bedroom. "We can prepare, and we can know we're going to kick his ass when we find him. But we can't let Olin hang over our heads every moment of every day. If we do, doesn't that kind of mean he's already won?"

She sat beside me on the bed, and I looked up at her. Her big eyes, her slightly wild hair.

I wanted to be like her in so many ways. Wild and free and outspoken.

"You're right," I said, because it really hit me in that moment. "We can't keep letting him hang over our heads. We have to get back to doing what we do. That's how we get stronger. That's how we win in the end."

She gave me a little smile, and then her eyes shifted over my shoulder.

I looked up to see Nathaniel walk in the room.

"Looks like you two got everything accomplished here," he said.

"Now you get to do the fun part with all the stairs," Mary-Beth teased him.

Nathaniel just laughed. And even though Mary-Beth acted like she was checking out, she still helped us carry all of the boxes down the stairs and into the truck we had rented.

It was strange, packing up all of my things from the only bedroom I'd ever occupied. I'd spent my entire life in that room. And here I was, twenty years old, moving out for the first time, straight into my own home.

It was sad. Bittersweet. But I also felt incredibly proud.

Dad said he had a staff meeting at the school and apologized that he couldn't be there to help. But really, I think he couldn't stand to watch it as I packed my things up and moved out.

I truly couldn't think about that part, that he was going to be alone in the house.

"Have fun settling in," Mary-Beth said as we loaded up the last box. "And get ready for the invasion in two days. You sure you can handle me all day, every day?"

"I'll take you every second, every moment," I said as I stepped forward and wrapped my arms around her. She hugged me back tightly, and I was incredibly grateful for her friendship. "Thank you."

"Don't thank me yet," she said as she patted my back before letting me go. With a wink, she turned and walked back toward her dorm.

"Ready?" Nathaniel asked.

I looked back at the house. I knew I was being dramatic. I would be back all the time. I was literally moving a three-minute drive away. But it still felt like closing a chapter.

"Yeah," I said, my voice sounding a little thick and husky.

We climbed into the truck and Nathaniel set off down the road.

"You know," I said. "I don't think I've ever seen you drive before. Who taught you how to drive as a teenager?"

Nathaniel looked over at me, looking slightly sheepish. "Myself. I, uh…me and this other boy at the group home would go out at night and hotwire cars that had been left unlocked. We would drive all over town, being idiots. We always returned the cars, and we were careful not to damage them. Just about anything that went wrong in that town got blamed on the boys' home, which was true half the time. But, after I got out of juvenile the last time, I put myself through the driving test and got my license. I've used it…maybe a dozen times since I got it," he said with a laugh.

I shook my head and chuckled. "Not that I should be laughing. I haven't driven much more since I got my own license. Since we never had an extra car, and everything here is within walking distance." I blinked, looking down the road as the house came into view. "We're going to have to buy a car, Nathaniel."

He looked over at me, being careful as he navigated through the gate, doing the passcode. "We?" he asked cautiously.

I smiled as he pulled up to the garage, which was now attached to the house. We opened the door, and Nathaniel carefully backed in.

I reached for his hand and ignored my things, instead pulling him inside the house.

Brent made the call to me last night. The house was finished. I was free to move in.

So, for the first time, I walked in, ready to settle into my new home.

It was beautiful. And stunning and perfect.

The rest of the furniture had been delivered yesterday. Cozy couches dominated the great room. The huge dining table sat beneath the chandelier. There were dishes in the cupboard and pots and pans.

It was entirely ready to move in to.

I walked Nathaniel and I to the great big window that looked out over the ocean. I turned to him and laced my fingers through his, looking up into his beautiful face. "I think its finally time for us to talk."

He looked down at me, and even though those words are rarely good between couples, I felt excited. And I loved that he seemed excited and open. He nodded. "I think it is time."

"We broke up because we couldn't see eye to eye when it came to handling confrontation," I said. And I felt a little more unsteady, thinking about that time and all the circumstances that pushed us to that point.

"Things are a little different now," Nathaniel said, voicing my own thoughts. He brought our hands up between us, looking at them laced together. "School is over. We have our own circles and we dived headfirst into creating our own lives. And…seeing Olin put his hands on you…"

There was a dark look on Nathaniel's face. I felt all of the muscles in his body tightening a bit.

He shook his head. "I thought I had locked away that part of myself for good. I thought I would eternally have control over it. But when Olin hurt you, it snapped.

My control fractured. And I realized that I've been keeping a chokehold on a part of who I am for years now."

"Nathaniel, I don't want you to feel like you have to fight bullies every day…" I started to say.

He shook his head. "I'm not saying that. I just mean that…there are going to be battles in life that I'm going to have to fight. But I am not the boy trying to survive any longer. I'm not just fighting to protect myself anymore. I have you to fight for, Margot. I have Mary-Beth and Borden and Poppy. Marie, Julie. Dorian and John. And Arthur. I think the other night I realized that maybe I have to look at it as a gift. I will protect those I love. And that's you most of all, Margot."

I reached up and placed a hand on the back of his head, bringing his forehead to mine. "I love you so much, Nathaniel." My words quivered because I felt them so deeply. My hands shook because they were filling me to the absolute brim. "I think we just had to have a rocky road figuring ourselves out. We had things so easy in the beginning. And I'm kind of grateful for all the stumbling blocks because they made me recognize and appreciate what we are. I want to be with you, Nathaniel. I'm done being in this limbo of questioning what we are. I'm all in."

A smile pulled in one corner of his mouth, and something fluttered in my chest.

My brain and my heart were utterly confused when

Nathaniel reached into his pocket, and he slowly lowered one knee to the floor.

In his hand, Nathaniel held a ring. It was a simple gold band, set with an emerald-cut diamond.

I sucked in a breath as my eyes rose back up to Nathaniel's.

"Margot, I've been absolutely astounded by you from the moment I first laid eyes on you," he said, and I loved the happiness that was flooding his face. "You're the smartest person I know and the most determined and dedicated. I truly can't imagine my life without you. I'm ready to move forward. I'm all in."

The air seemed to still and the moment seemed suspended in the air. And for just a moment, I stared into Nathaniel's green eyes. And I saw everything laying before us in the future.

"Margot," Nathaniel breathed out in a gentle, low tone, "will you marry me?"

Those four words rattled in my brain and in my chest, and two very conflicting thoughts kept warring inside of me.

I was only twenty years old. Nathaniel was only twenty-three.

Yet we were standing inside this mansion I owned. We were about to launch our own school.

Why would I ever let a number define any decision?

Because the other part of me was screaming yes, yes,

yes, because Nathaniel and I belonged together, no matter what was thrown in our way.

"Yes!" I basically screamed, before I launched myself at him, wrapping my arms behind his head and pressing my lips so tightly to his, neither of us could breathe.

Nathaniel stood but did not break the kiss. He lifted me right off my feet, clutching me to him like I was his last dying breath.

I backed away just a little bit, and with a happy chuckle, Nathaniel looked down. And he slid that beautiful, perfect ring onto my finger.

I looked up at him, and suddenly tears were stinging my eyes. I reached up, brushing my fingers into his hair. "It's all coming together," I said. "It's perfect. I can't…" I shook my head. "I can't believe that we're suddenly here."

"We're in this together," Nathaniel said. "All of it."

He leaned down, and gently, he pressed his lips to mine.

Fiancé. Nathaniel was my fiancé.

Just yesterday, we were still a question mark that we didn't know how to answer when asked. And now we were committing the rest of our lives together.

And I didn't have one ounce of hesitation in me about it.

"Come on," Nathaniel said, whispering against my lips. "I have a surprise for you."

I probably looked like a lunatic because I was smiling

so big. But my heart leapt into my throat, and I happily bounded after Nathaniel.

Holding my hand, he led me to the master bedroom, covering my eyes as we walked up to it.

"You ready?" he whispered in my ear.

"Absolutely," I said.

Nathaniel uncovered my eyes, and my hands went straight to my heart.

There was a massive four-poster bed in the middle of the room. Huge and grand. It was covered in a ridiculously fluffy pale green comforter. And there were ten pillows on it, set up in perfect order.

"I love it," I said, reaching back and grabbing his hand as I pulled him forward. I turned as we got to the bed, taking his mouth with mine. We tumbled into the bed, and I just imagined all the nights we were going to spend here together.

Maybe we would wait until the wedding night. We were both a little old fashioned in some ways. And while we never outright talked about that aspect, we'd made it this far. By this point, I took it as a bit of a challenge.

And now, getting a small preview of what was to come, I could hardly wait.

Who needed six months to plan a wedding? Maybe we could pull this together in two.

CHAPTER TWENTY-FIVE

I got another surprise that night.

Dad threw us an engagement party. Nathaniel had, of course, gotten Dad's blessing. And that night, we had dinner at my house, and all of our closest friends were there. Even Poppy had arrived, bringing our newest mage recruit, a man in his mid-twenties by the name of Peter Wills.

They'd all been ecstatic about our engagement. For the first time ever, our news shocked Mary-Beth speechless, for an entire thirty seconds.

Cautiously, I'd watched Borden's expression. He'd kept a fairly blank face, but a small, controlled smile did curl on his lips after ten seconds. He kept his distance somewhat throughout the rest of the night.

But still, it was a perfect night and a perfect end to the day.

Over the next two days, we moved everyone in. The house had plenty of bedrooms, so everyone had a place. Mary-Beth was on the opposite end of the house from my bedroom. Borden went in across the hall from her. Poppy next to that. Both Dorian and John had their own homes they would be staying in. But Peter and Marie and Julie all chose to move in. I'd even offered to Dad, but he had declined and said he couldn't leave the house he and Mom had purchased together.

And we moved Nathaniel right into the master bedroom.

It was sad, actually. Moving Nathaniel out of the solarium. He'd made that space himself, rebuilt it after years of abandonment. That had been his sacred space.

When I voiced my sadness over it, Nathaniel had put his hands on my hips and said, "I have loved this place, Margot. But it also represents some loneliness for me. A time when I had no friends and no family. Look at everything I have now. Friends, family. A wonderful fiancée. Where else in the world would I possibly want to be but in that spectacular house with you?"

His words melted me, and I hadn't questioned him further.

It was an adjustment, all of us actually living together. We'd spent mass amounts of time with one another, but truly living in the same household was different. We had to figure out how to share groceries and house chores.

But it was genuinely really wonderful. There was always someone to talk to. There were deep conversations and insides jokes. The house was full of depth and laughter.

We were truly becoming a family.

On May eighteenth, we were all gathered together for dinner. Poppy had cooked, something traditionally Scottish. It tasted wonderful, but didn't smell that great. We'd been talking excitedly about the coming few days.

In the letters we'd sent out, we'd instructed our new students to come to this address on June twentieth to start their first semester.

"I need to tell you all something," Borden said as he spoke up. Everyone looked down the table at him. "I've decided to travel with Poppy, testing for new recruits."

That information dropped into the pit of my stomach like a stone-cold potato.

"Poppy can test passengers on her flights, but with her sometimes extended layovers, it provides ample time to go out and find others," he said. And I knew Borden well enough now to see that something was amiss in his eyes. This wasn't necessarily what he wanted. But as my eyes drifted down to my left hand and saw the ring on my finger, I thought that perhaps I understood. "We need to grow our family. There is safety in numbers. And perhaps while I am out, I will find Olin, and can put an end to our wondering."

There were seven beats of silence as everyone digested the information he had just dropped on us.

"Are you sure?" I asked, needing to be the first one to speak. "You know you are needed here, in so many different ways."

Borden's eyes met mine, and in them, I saw the pain he'd been hiding so well for so long now. "I'm sure. But thank you, Margot, for everything."

I hated that it sounded like a goodbye. "You know this will always be your home, right? Your room will be waiting for you when you get back, just like the rest of us."

Borden nodded, offering a smile that looked sadder than I would have hoped.

"I'm sure you'll do great work then," I moved on, because there was nothing else I could do. "And while we're making announcements, I guess I have one of my own."

I sat up a little taller, fittingly seated at the head of the table. Everyone stopped eating, and all eyes fixed on me.

"As you all know, our next and first official semester starts in two days," I said. "And I've finally come to a decision on a name for the school, and the house."

My heart raced in anticipation, but it was a good feeling. "And that is Nightingale Academy."

I looked over at Nathaniel, and the shock on his face was adorable. "You're the one that started this entire resurrection."

"But this was your vision, Margot," he pointed out.

I shook my head. "It was our vision. And our future. Besides, you're the one with the coolest last name."

Everyone laughed at that. "She does have you there," Mary-Beth said, raising a glass in toasting.

"To the Nightingale Academy," Poppy said, also raising her glass.

Nathaniel looked at me one more time, and I saw something in his eyes. Appreciation. Pride. Excitement. And I knew I had made exactly the right choice.

In two days time, new students would arrive. They would move into the school. We would begin teaching classes. Magic would be an everyday thing. It was already becoming our normal here, within these walls where we were safe, and we could always be ourselves.

This was the dawn of what I knew would be a beautiful age. And I couldn't wait to greet it with open arms.

There was a quick knock on the door and half of all of us got up to get it. But when I heard the door swing open without much waiting for anyone to answer, I knew it was my dad.

I smiled as I walked to the entry.

But when I turned the corner and the front door came into view, all of my organs dropped to my feet, and every ounce of my blood evaporated.

"Mom?" I breathed out.

She looked up at me, standing in front of my Dad.

Her eyes had aged, and there were a few gray strands in her hair. But that was unmistakably my mother.

"Hello, Margot," she said in an emotional whisper.

THE END OF BOOK THREE

ABOUT THE AUTHOR

Keary Taylor is the USA TODAY bestselling author of over thirty titles, encompassing paranormal, sci-fi, and contemporary romance. She grew up along the foothills of the Rocky Mountains where, from a young age, she started creating imaginary worlds and daring characters who always fell in love. She now lives on a tiny island in the Pacific Northwest with her husband and their two children. She continues to have an overactive imagination that frequently keeps her up at night.

ABOUT THE AUTHOR

Keary Taylor is the USA TODAY bestselling author of over thirty titles, encompassing paranormal, sci-fi, and contemporary romance. She grew up along the foothills of the Rocky Mountains where, from a young age, she started creating imaginary worlds and daring characters who always fell in love. She now lives on a tiny island in the Pacific Northwest with her husband and their two children. She continues to have an overactive imagination that frequently keeps her up at night.

Printed in Great Britain
by Amazon